CIVILIZATIONS

Michael Searle

New York   Toronto   London   Auckland   Sydney
Mexico City   New Delhi   Hong Kong   Buenos Aires

ISBN 0-439-73382-0

Designed by MADA Design, Inc.

12 11 10 9 8 7 6 5 4 3 2 1   5 6 7 8 9/0

Printed in the U.S.A.
First printing, October 2005

tHe anCIent WaR

The earth shook and ended a thousand years of peace.

Before the Great Explosion, the five civilizations respected each other, content to let neighboring cultures develop and flourish.

After the devastating earthquakes, the five civilizations were thrown into chaos.

The underground caverns, home to the Darkness creatures, collapsed and fell into ruins.

Fire and Nature creatures scrambled on the surface to survive the shifting landmasses.

While the seas boiled, tremors toppled the Water's undersea citadels.

Up in the sky, only the Light civilization remained untouched . . . for now.

DARK DECEIT

The first eruptions hurt the Darkness civilization the most. Already a devastated region, the Great Explosion further destroyed what little the Darkness creatures had. Fortunately, the earthquakes opened a crack to the surface world. Left with few choices, the Dark Lords decided to invade the forests above and claim a new land for the Darkness nation.

The Dark Lords wanted nothing but absolute victory, so they sent forth millions of parasite worms to swarm the land. These vile worms ate everything in their path and even converted corpses into food and shelter. They struck at the heart of the Nature realm, Niofa Forest, and spoiled the most beautiful of Nature's woods to make it their own.

Darkness' General Dark Fiend attacks Nature's Niofa Forest.

1   **36**   **37**

Great Explosion starts Ancient War.   Fire and Water nations attack each other.

NATURE'S REVOLT

Deep in the woods, Nature's Silver Hair tribe heard the screams of Niofa Forest. Horrified, but determined to stop the wave of destruction, the Silver Hair tribe marched forth and fought the Darkness worms. The battle raged, and the Nature creatures, cold steel in hand, destroyed the worms that had poisoned their land.

The Dark Lords, however, had a second, even deadlier wave of troops. They summoned forth the demon command, and the superpowerful bone warriors crushed all of the Silver Hair tribe except their leader, Silver Fist. With the forests on the brink of annihilation, the beast folk's dying cries stirred Nature's great protectors, the giants. The two civilizations' most powerful races now fought for the ultimate prize — survival.

Silver Fist forms Silver Hair tribe.

Light aids Nature. Darkness recruits Fire.

40

43

204

Nature's giants awake.

FLOOD WARNING

The Water creatures wept for their broken cities while their Cyber Lords devised a plan of attack on the land. They would have to seize territory to start a new civilization, and their scouts chose the primitive Fire civilization as the easiest conquest.

All the Cyber Lords' combat simulations, however, had not factored in the Fire civilization's advanced technology, resurrected from the ancient days. When they stormed the Fire realm's beaches and assaulted the cities among the volcanoes, the dragonoids' molten-powered weapons sizzled the liquid people, and the rock beasts splattered the seaside invaders.

Survivors attack from their Lost City.

211　　**345**　　**367**

Light withdraws army to protect home from Fire.　　Darkness battles back against Survivors.

BURNING BRIGHT

Unable to accept defeat, Water's Cyber Lords unlocked two of the 12 forbidden programs from their secret database. These programs transformed some of their chosen creatures into superior evolutions. Armed with the new technology and a greater understanding of Fire's weapons, the Cyber Lords' army launched a more fearsome invasion.

The villages on the outskirts of the Fire civilization began to fall. Either overrun by the Evolution-led liquid people or trampled along the shores by the massive leviathans, the Fire creatures were forced to retreat farther inland.

Yet again, the Cyber Lords underestimated the people of Fire. Though humans and dragonoids had hated each other for centuries, they banded together to fight this greater threat. The combined might of the Fire civilization forced the remaining Water creatures back into the ocean.

Survivor army finally defeated.

Fire's wyverns harm Light civilization.

441

458

504

Light invents world's first invincible cannon.

LET THERE BE LIGHT

The Light civilization once had the heavens to itself. High up in the clouds, its cities shone with shiny alloy metals and shimmering energy fields, and the Light creatures lived a happy and peaceful life.

It would not last.

Seeing the beautiful forests under siege from the creatures of Darkness, the creatures of the Light civilization decided that they should order the chaos in the world. They teamed up with Nature and added their technological might to the battle below.

Overmatched, the Darkness civilization called on the Fire creatures as allies.

With the Water civilization staying neutral and taking its opportunities from either side, the new battle lines had been drawn: Light and Nature versus Darkness and Fire.

The world would never be the same again.

Nature's mystery totems invade Darkness civilization.

508   **539**   **545**

Light destroys Fire's volcanic fortress and wakes dragons.

Fire and Nature form a secret alliance.

LIGHT CIVILIZATION

WATER CIVILIZATION

DUEL MASTERS

NATURE CIVILIZATION

DARKNESS CIVILIZATION

LIGHT CIVILIZATION

They were once seen as gods, and their most powerful defenders are called "angels." Because they live up in the sky, the Light creatures have the respect or fear of the other four civilizations, and they have taken advantage of their past security to build a magnificent empire in the clouds.

Like the civilization's stunning buildings, many of the Light beings also have shiny, symmetrical forms and hover in the air. The Light creatures believe in concepts like order, obedience, and the ability of each individual to make a difference.

Though they prefer peace, they can bring potent weapons to the battlefield, including laser beams, gravity fields, and teleportation devices. When an overpowering army of berserkers, gladiators, guardians, and mecha thunders heads your way, by the time you see the light, it may be too late.

ANGEL COMMAND

The most powerful soldiers in the Light civilization require so much energy to power up that the angel command units have only been activated twice — ever! When they enter battle, these warriors defend the Light colonies with weapons that levitate around them. Each member of the angel command is unique in appearance, disciplined in destructive capabilities, and guided by thoughts of war.

BERSERKERS

The Light's primary invasion force attacks until it destroys the enemy or the enemy destroys it. Each berserker will not waver, rest, or retreat until it completes the task at hand. With an armorlike skin made up of pieces of alloy metal connected by a special energy field, these large creatures — some as big as a massive battleship! — cut through living targets with their light sabers and relentless fury.

GUARDIANS

As you might guess from the name, these defenders rally to protect the Light civilization once a threat has been detected. Shaped like birds for better mobility, the guardians can range in size from a car to a tank and attack with a hawk's deadly accuracy. They are always on call, so as soon as the alarm sounds, Light's guardians automatically swoop in to save the day.

INITIATES

There are more initiates than any other Light race, mainly because the light bringers use them as servants and have created them over the years in many different shapes and sizes. These artificial life forms stay frozen in a holding mode until called upon by their masters to perform certain tasks. They're very good at assisting the light bringers, but aren't known for their fighting skills.

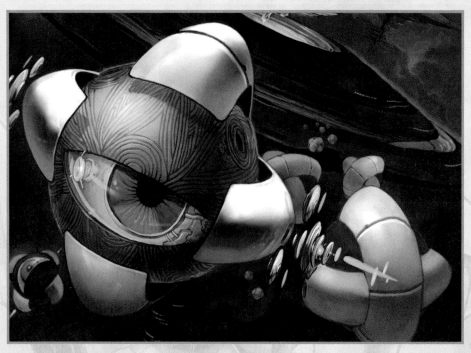

LIGHT BRINGERS

The masters of the Light civilization live in Central City's core, but they are merely clones of the great leaders who came before them. Within their innermost chamber, a sacred archive holds the data of every light bringer who has ever existed. The few dozen remaining light bringers power these terminals, and as long as the master database survives, they can truly never die.

MECHA THUNDERS

A raging tornado rips through an army and scatters creatures and weaponry for miles. For destruction like that, the Light civilization calls forth the creatures tapped into the elements, the mecha thunders. Part human and part machine, the mecha thunders surround themselves with storm clouds and lightning, and create natural disasters by controlling the weather.

RAINBOW PHANTOMS

The most spectacular-looking Light creatures have bodies made of a fabriclike energy that shimmers like a rainbow. The specially designed creatures can scout out an area and report back enemy activity. If engaged in battle, rainbow phantoms' energy patterns distract their foes and allow them to dodge, deflect, and return enemy fire easily. They can also turn invisible to avoid detection.

STARLIGHT TREES

You won't see too many trees around the Light civilization's high-tech world. The Light culture, instead, relies on metal, computers, and powerful energy to survive. However, the Light creatures do plant starlight trees around the city to serve as natural barriers. Starlight trees emit a magnetic field that repels enemies, plus they absorb poisons and harmful gases.

MIAR, COMET ELEMENTAL

It was created to beat the dragons.

After the Ancient War came to the Light civilization and the primeval creatures of destruction, the dragons, had risen again from the ashes, the light bringers built Miar, Comet Elemental and the rest of the angel command.

To combat the winged beasts, the light bringers harnessed the sun's power directly into their new soldiers. The amount of energy needed to power Miar equals the entire output of a Light city for a whole month!

As the light bringers watched from high overhead, the mighty battle between the angel command and dragons shook the very foundation of the earth. Miar learned to heat up the atmosphere and drain that energy to fire laser beams that annihilated anything and everything in its path.

But Miar was growing too strong, and so the light bringers shut down the colossus. Now, its doomsday touch will be released only in times of absolute desperation.

Phal Eega, Dawn Guardian
5
GUARDIAN

illus. Daisuke Izuka

CREATURE

• When you put this creature into the battle zone, you may return a spell from your graveyard to your hand.

"Like the sun, I'm just getting warmed up."

4000

©2004 Wizards of the Coast/
Shogakukan/Mitsui-Kids ★ 8/55

Legend claims that the Light's guardian creatures are not flesh and blood, but machine. Those that have watched them on the battlefield swear that living creatures could not react with such speed and strength. Phal Eaga, one of the most powerful guardians, leads the Light army's defenses with a suit of armor that sucks energy directly from the sun and generates shields that can block an enemy traveling up to 2,900 miles per hour!

In battle, Phal Eaga organizes the other guardians into a "curtain" — a wall of guardians linked together by bands of heat. While the other guardians concentrate on deflecting enemy attacks, Phal Eaga channels its sun power to the guardians already intent on the combat before them. Amid the clash of weapons and force blasts, you can see the magnificent Phal Eaga spread its wings so that its feathers can absorb the maximum amount of energy and spread it to the rest of the Light army.

Guardians
Protection of the light bringers and the Light cities falls on the shoulders of these battle-tested creatures.

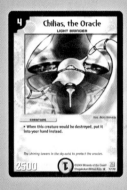

Light Bringers
These ancient beings run the civilization from the Light's massive database.

Angel Command
The Light's mega weapons have only been activated twice — they're that powerful!

Rainbow Phantoms
Although they fight well, these troops can turn invisible and prove the Light's best scouts.

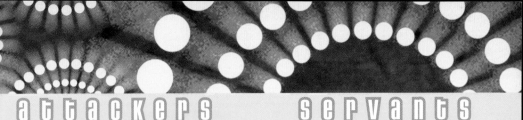

Berserkers
These never-say-die warriors are the Light's primary invasion force.

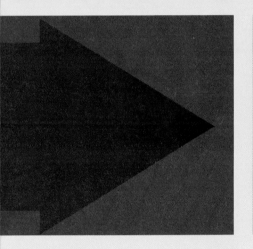

Initiates
The light bringers created these beings for everyday purposes like cleaning and transportation.

Mecha Thunders
When the Light commanders want to destroy large enemy armies, they call in these weather manipulators.

water civilization

Deep in the ocean, past the transparent buildings made of solidified seawater, a giant tower shaped like a spiraling DNA strand holds the Cyber Lords, rulers of the Water civilization. The great Cyber Lords control the water beings through technology — many of the water creatures have a computer chip installed in their bodies. This chip enables the water creatures to communicate telepathically, but it also gives the Cyber Lords the power to instruct those same creatures to do their bidding.

The Water society prefers knowledge and study over violence and warfare. If an army threatens their shores, the beings of the Water civilization will rely on strategies and tactics to beat the enemy, not overpowering might. They may not be the strongest warriors, but they do have technology on their side. Some of the more talented water creatures can shape the seawater around them into weapons, armor, and even vehicles.

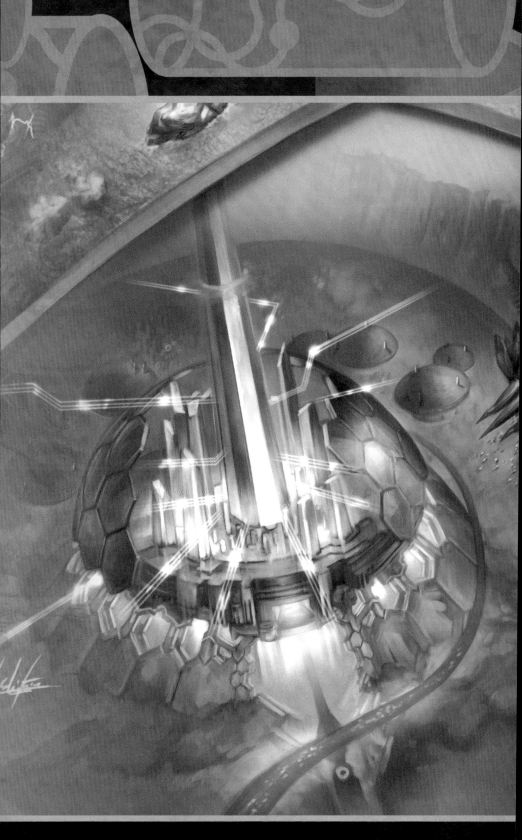

CYBER CLUSTERS

Water's liquid people use the cyber clusters as walking forts. The robotic shellfish look like crabs, shrimps, starfish, and hermit crabs, but you don't want to mistake them for the normal variety. Whenever a cyber cluster gets attacked, it emits bright sparks and supersonic or electromagnetic waves that disrupt enemy attacks and warn the liquid people that danger is near.

CYBER LORDS

The masters of the Water civilization look like babies and might as well be infants when it comes to hand-to-hand combat. Cyber Lords have little physical strength, so they have developed their minds instead. Each lord has a large computer chip installed in its head, and with the help of that technology, its brain waves can control other creatures and manipulate objects.

CYBER VIRUSES

Created by the Cyber Lords, these tiny creatures — the largest no bigger than a worm — can infiltrate any equipment. A cyber virus can scout out a satellite, destroy a radio, or rewrite a computer program. It can just as easily disrupt a creature's thought patterns as cause a machine to malfunction. The Water civilization relies on these secret attacks to stay ahead of the other races.

EARTH EATERS

Water creatures aren't just limited to the seas. Earth eaters are huge bio-weapons that the beings of the Water civilization activate to patrol their shores and to attack enemy territory. The earth eaters devour chunks of land, which digests in their stomach and fuels their internal fusion generators. Because of earth eaters' destructive nature, Water creatures stay far away and let the monsters do their work alone.

race recon

GEL FISH

With bodies made out of water and wires, these constructions can transform from liquid to solid to gas. Their many shapes allow the Cyber Lords to employ gel fish as weapons, defense, or transportation. Gel fish consume everything around them in the water, and they have been known to grow big enough to destroy an entire city by eating it.

LEVIATHANS

The Cyber Lords do not control the Water civilization's most powerful race, the leviathans. The leviathans are so big that they have been mistaken for islands, but it's the leviathans' high intelligence that prevents the Cyber Lords from dominating them. The tamer leviathans have huge weapons attached to them, or, in the case of the real giants, entire cities have been built on their backs.

LIQUID PEOPLE

The liquid people obey orders well and have become the main fighting force for the Water civilization. Their bodies are encased in a fluid that can shift into many different forms, making them ideal for both offense and defense. Chips inside the liquid people's heads allow them to speak through thoughts, which gives them the advantage of swift action in battle.

SEA HACKERS

An aggressive race of Water creatures, the sea hackers resemble squid, octopi, and the stranger fish at the bottom of the ocean. They will eat anything, including machinery and armor. As a result, many sea hackers have mutated and grown a metallic exterior. Sea hackers defend their territory with a combination of tentacles and electric shocks.

AQUA DEFORMER

8

Aqua Deformer
LIQUID PEOPLE

illus. Dustmoss

CREATURE

- When you put this creature into the battle zone, return 2 cards from your mana zone to your hand. Then your opponent chooses 2 cards in his mana zone and returns them to his hand.

Nothing is quite what it seems.

3000

©2004 Wizards of the Coast/
Shogakukan/Mitsui-Kids ★ 13/55

It can take any form — clam, shark, or killer whale. The Cyber Lords designed this highly intelligent android to morph into whatever body best suits its environment, and in most cases, the shape it takes is intended to scare its enemies into retreat before the battle even begins.

On land, an aqua deformer can gather water from every source — mud, bog slime, fresh water — and cascade that water into a great wave which washes away the terrain. It also coats itself in dark mud to look like a monster from the deep and to shield itself from the sun's rays, thus lasting twice as long on land than any other Water creature.

Though a formidable physical fighter, the Aqua Deformer also brings psychological warfare to the battlefield. During combat, it scans for an opponent's weakness and learns from an enemy's every move. When defeated, the Aqua Deformer rises again next battle armed with the information it learned from its loss. You cannot defeat it the same way twice.

KING PONITAS

How do you fight something that measures 17 miles across and has lived for 500 years? The Water civilization's enemies still haven't come up with a good response to this king of the leviathans.

Allying with King Ponitas, the Cyber Lords devised an attack strategy, called "Cyber Blitz Tactics," that can reduce almost any enemy nation to rubble in hours. First, the Water creatures surround the enemy area and flood the land. As the raging waters surge over the landmass, the leviathans, led by King Ponitas, thrash their bodies from the sea to the land and crush everything they fall upon. Each leviathan leap destroys entire enemy regiments and their fortifications in seconds.

However, King Ponitas lends more than its massive body to the battle. Its song can reach more than a thousand miles in every direction, and when it signals, all Water creatures in hearing range converge in a surprise attack that no one ever sees coming.

water technology

The Tower: Shaped like a giant DNA strand, the home of the Cyber Lords holds environmental living cylinders and the heart of the Water civilization's technology, the Ultracomputer.

Cyber Virus: As tiny as a piece of plankton, a cyber virus can slip past enemy defenses, infect a computer system, and deactivate its core programming in minutes.

Fusion Engine: These reactors power the giant earth eaters that the Cyber Lords send onto the land to eat away at enemy defenses. The engine is based on ancier technology rediscovered by the Cyber Lords.

3 Clone Factory

SPELL

- Return up to 2 cards from your mana zone to your hand.

The factory works day and night, laboring at endeavors best left unknown.

©2004 Wizards of the Coast/
Shogakukan/Mitsui-Kids 21/55

Clone Factory:
The Water civilization can produce creatures for war and servitude with this machine deep in the heart of Central City.

Computer Chips:
Most Water creatures have a special computer chip installed in their brain, which gives them telepathic communication and access to a wealth of database knowledge.

2 Emeral
CYBER LORD

CREATURE

- When you put this creature into the battle zone, you may add a card from your hand to your shields face down. If you do, choose one of your shields and put it into your hand. You can't use the "shield trigger" ability of that shield.

"If you think I'm good at this, watch me play video games."

1000

©2004 Wizards of the Coast/
Shogakukan/Mitsui-Kids 19/55

6 Hydro Hurricane

SPELL

- For each light creature you have in the battle zone, you may choose a card in your opponent's mana zone and return it to his hand.
- For each darkness creature you have in the battle zone, you may choose one of your opponent's creatures in the battle zone and return it to his hand.

©2004 Wizards of the Coast/
Shogakukan/Mitsui-Kids 23/55

Secret Energy:
Only a few individuals know the secret power of the Water civilization: The Cyber Lords tap into the very ocean current itself to draw forth their greatest energies.

Seawater Weapons:
Many Water creatures can conjure weapons from the water or create exoskeletal armor from the metal remains of creatures that have fallen before them in combat.

4 Thought Probe

SPELL

- Shield trigger *(When this spell is put into your hand from your shield zone, you may cast it immediately for no cost.)*
- When you cast this spell, if your opponent has 3 or more creatures in the battle zone, draw 3 cards.

©2004 Wizards of the Coast/
Shogakukan/Mitsui-Kids 20/55

13 Invincible Technology

SPELL

- Search your deck. You may take any number of cards from your deck, show those cards to your opponent, and put them into your hand. Then shuffle your deck.

The Acashic Database holds the secrets of the universe. After centuries of searching, the Cyber Lords have at last found a clue to deciphering it.

©2005 Wizards of the Coast/
Shogakukan/Mitsui-Kids 47/110

Acashic Database:
Legend has it this database holds the secrets of the universe, and after centuries of work, the Cyber Lords finally have found a clue to deciphering it.

Steam Star:
Placed at the bottom of the ocean to monitor volcanic vents and collect steam, they can use the steam as an energy source or a weapon.

2 Steam Star
CYBER VIRUS

CREATURE

The Cyber Lords deploy them at volcanic vents on the bottom of the ocean. They monitor the superheated steam, collect it, and—when necessary—use it as a weapon.

1000

©2005 Wizards of the Coast/
Shogakukan/Mitsui-Kids 60/110

Darkness Civilization

Poison, disease, and death shape the existence of each Darkness creature. The gases that swirl around the Darkness civilization poison those that have not adapted, so the creatures of the dark wear special masks to cover and protect their faces. Disease has ravaged the skin of races like the living dead and parasite worms. Since death has replaced life for most Darkness creatures, and the duration of their existence grows shorter and shorter, those that haven't gone crazy seek the power of immortality to extend their time.

Many Darkness creatures suit up in bone armor, and most, after living in the dark for so long, are blind. That doesn't mean they are powerless. Some Darkness races control dead bodies and turn them into zombies, while other races have been experimented on and have merged with different animals or even garbage. The most powerful creatures of all, the Dark Lords, rule the whole underworld through their secret, corrupt magic.

BRAIN JACKERS

These spiderlike creatures wouldn't last two seconds out on the battlefield alone. Brain jackers aren't durable creatures, but their big advantage lies in their ability to control dead bodies. Once an enemy creature dies, a brain jacker will slip over the head of the corpse and inject its legs into the creature's central nervous system, thus taking complete control of all functions.

CHIMERAS

Bear, elephant, tiger, wolverine — a chimera can be any one of these, and most likely will be a combination of all of them. Long ago, the Dark Lords experimented on the poor creatures and changed them into fearsome monsters that merged the bone spurs, fangs, and poisons of whatever animals they could trap. Now they look intimidating and deadly!

DARK LORDS

Besides holding the greatest technologies and magic of the Darkness kingdom, the Dark Lords own all the energy resources, toxic gas factories, and cures for certain diseases. If you want any of these things, the Dark Lords require only one thing: complete and utter obedience. While they appear to be human, no one knows what forms lie behind their beautiful masks.

DEATH PUPPETS

The Dark Lords created these artificial creatures as disposable weapons, but they have a unique talent for staying alive. During combat, death puppets will sneak attack an enemy, but if the odds look grim, they will crumple to look like broken toys. If they are injured, they will stitch the wound; thus, many death puppets appear with patchwork skin and mixed body parts.

DEMON COMMAND

The Darkness race with the fewest members ends up the most powerful. The Dark Lords built the demon command creatures as their civilization's strongest weapons. Each demon command creature takes a unique form, such as a lion or bird, and gains that animal's abilities. They are also crafted from bone, so decay and corrosion do not harm them.

GHOSTS

Darkness' ghosts are creatures that unsuccessfully abandoned their bodies in the search for eternal life. Now they're stuck in foglike bodies that resemble the creatures they were before they died. Ghosts cannot live without power from the Dark Lords, and they have such a hatred for flesh that they will terrorize any living creature until it goes insane.

HEDRIANS

Born of sludge and ooze, the hedrians have made the best of being stuck in the sewers. In half-liquid form, they travel the polluted waterways under the Darkness civilization and alter their bodies to pick up garbage along the way. It's not just disgustingly decorative, either. Hedrians collect waste to fashion into all sorts of weapons to use against their enemies.

LIVING DEAD

The living dead's ancestors infected themselves with a special virus strain to try and achieve immortality. They failed and became zombielike creatures that have been driven nearly mad with a constant hunger. As the main force in the Darkness army, they can prove very deadly — injured enemies can be infected with the virus and turn into more living dead!

GENERAL DARK FIEND

In the Ancient War, General Dark Fiend led the demon command against Nature's strongest tribe and shattered it to pieces. For this victory, along with many others, the General was awarded one of the top positions in the Darkness hierarchy. The General wears blackened bone armor and a regal red cape, and when the General stands alongside its fellow Dark Lords, it towers over them.

General Dark Fiend cuts through the enemy with a mighty sword in one hand and tendrils of shadow in the other. At the start of each battle, the General's war cry sends the troops of Darkness into a battle frenzy, mostly because they fear the General more than the enemy. Should any segments of the General's armor fall off during the skirmish, the General's minions will battle each other for the privilege of returning the piece. Of course, the lucky minion seldom lives to enjoy the General's favor.

The Dark Lords gathered the most ruthless creatures from every race and turned those creatures into the demon command, and they chose Vashuna to train them in the art of hand-to-hand combat. Before the demon command waded into war, they developed a keen sense of battle tactics and a hunger for violence. Vashuna gave them discipline and the skill to stay alive.

Vashuna, a master of the twin swords that he wields, swings his weapons so quickly that they cannot be seen. None can match Vashuna's agility and expert swordsmanship. Though he barely moves, approaching enemies seem to simply fall to pieces before him. This swirl of blades also has a hypnotizing effect on opposing creatures. At first, he rotates the swords slowly, as if in a dance, and quickly speeds up to mesmerize nearby foes. Before they realize it, Vashuna's foes have walked close enough that they will never take another step again.

SURVIVAL OF THE FITTEST

Ballom, Master of Death
Strength: 12,000 Power
Race: Demon command
Survival Skills: No creature challenges this monstrosity and lives to brag about it.

Zagaan, Knight of Darkness
Strength: 7,000 Power
Race: Demon command
Survival Skills: A fearsome skeleton that eats almost everything it can reach.

Volcano Smog, Deceptive Shade
Strength: 5,000 Power
Race: Ghost
Survival Skills: For a ghost, it packs a big punch.

Dark Clown
Strength: 6,000 Power
Race: Brain jacker
Survival Skills: As a blocker, it never attacks.

Poison Worm
Strength: 4,000 Power
Race: Parasite worm
Survival Skills: It's not a tasty snack for those without heavy-duty defenses.

Gigastand
Strength: 3,000 Power
Race: Chimera
Survival Skills: It can withstand more punishment than normal creatures its size.

Writhing Bone Ghoul
Strength: 2,000 Power
Race: Living dead
Survival Skills: Its teeth hurt, but seldom kill.

Locomotiver
Strength: 1,000 Power
Race: Hedrian
Survival Skills: It moves quickly, but doesn't have a good track record for staying alive.

FIRE CIVILIZATION

Their hunger for destruction destroyed paradise.

During the Ancient War, the thriving Fire civilization pushed their experiments further and further until they discovered a massively powerful weapon, a weapon that turned the earth's molten lava into a deadly tool. Unfortunately for the Fire beings, the magma weapon caused a dramatic shift in the Earth's crust and shattered their cities. Gone were the technological marvels of the past, replaced by ash-spewing volcanoes and crippling earthquakes.

The Fire civilization rebuilt, and its people hardened. They now fought without mercy and continued until they annihilated their enemy and took all the enemy's possessions for themselves. A Fire creature will never surrender. It's better to die honorably than retreat and face shame after the battle. Because they like to show off, Fire creatures overdress for each battle, so much so that with all the armor and weapons, you might not recognize what's inside all that equipment.

ARMORED DRAGONS

Worshipped by the dragonoids as gods, the armored dragons top the list of the Fire civilization's most powerful creatures. Dragons are highly independent, with many different powers and personalities. Some will scorch a battlefield for the sake of a good time, while others prefer to stay hidden in the mountains meditating on the secrets of life.

ARMORED WYVERNS

They may look like dragons, but a dragon would never allow another creature to ride on its back! Dragonoids breed the armored wyverns as combat-trained mounts and will organize these creatures into formidable military squadrons in times of war. Once found wild roaming the land, wyverns are rarely seen outside a dragonoid training camp now.

ARMORLOIDS

Before the Ancient War, these human-created robots worked smoothly. Now, however, humans can't find new machine parts, and the robots can no longer repair themselves. They have begun to wear down. Only high-ranking humans know the codes to operate these machines of war, and the active armorloids rule the battlefield with ancient technology.

DRAGONOIDS

These lizardlike creatures think and breathe war. Over time, they have learned to ignite underground volcanic eruptions to use as bombs against their enemy targets. They mine iron and make gunpowder to turn themselves into living war weapons. Dragonoids oppose humans throughout the Fire civilization, as both sides attempt to seize control of the empire.

race recon

HUMANS

You will rarely see a human without his or her mask. From the time of adulthood, humans wear full suits of armor, and it is considered a dishonorable act to remove the armored mask in public. They choose many different adventurous jobs, such as armored warriors to protect people, treasure hunters to recover lost artifacts, and commanders to run the armorloids.

MACHINE EATERS

Want a motorized toy car or a working toothbrush? Go see the machine eaters. These childlike humanoids, only a foot high, know all there is to know about the ins and outs of machinery. In exchange for their great engineering skills, both humans and dragonoids invite machine eaters into their camps and allow them to play with broken and discarded spare parts.

ROCK BEASTS

Made of living rock, these beasts thrive in the Earth's steaming magma and actually drink the molten fluid to survive. As adults, they leave the magma and roam the land, some growing as big as a hill! Dragonoids have captured many rock beasts and trained them for battle as living fortresses that stomp and crush the enemy under their vast weight.

XENOPARTS

Unlike the powerful armorloids that were built to last, these machine eater-designed robots got stuck with the leftover parts. Cobbled together with whatever crazy combination was available at the time — gears, wrenches, vises, screws — xenopart creatures still prove useful in battle. The hovering robots can emit magnetic waves to disrupt opponents and repair broken machines.

LEGENDS OF FIRE

ARMORED WARRIOR QUELOS

You don't want to mess with a battle robot that can blast a crater a mile wide. Though it was built before the Ancient War, Armored Warrior Quelos's batteries are still going strong. Of course, the Fire creatures aren't always happy about that fact. If Quelos senses a threat, the robot will react with all its weaponry and combat programs. Should an ally be nearby at the time, it's just as likely to get hit by Quelos's friendly fire as it is a missile from enemy artillery.

Dragonoids play a dangerous game with armorloids such as Armored Warrior Quelos. Since dragonoids cannot control the armorloids, they run across a particular spot of terrain and draw the nearby robot's fire. The resulting explosion from the dragonoids' trick run splits open the earth and spills out precious metals and minerals that the race turns into tools, weapons, and shelter. One running mistake, though, and Armored Warrior Quelos improves its kill ratio yet again.

ÜBERDRAGON JABAHA

He was the first dragon to stir from his 10,000-year slumber. During the Ancient War, when the Darkness civilization's worms invaded and destroyed Nature's forest home, the destruction spread across the world and decimated the Fire realm as well. The disturbance awoke the ancient dragons, and Überdragon Jabaha rallied the dragons and led them into battle against the other civilizations. When Überdragon Jabaha had fallen asleep, the Fire realm had been lush trees and fertile valley. At the sight of the blasted landscape that was now the Fire civilization, Jabaha's rage fueled the destruction of enemy after enemy, even some as powerful as Water's leviathans and Light's angel command.

In combat, Überdragon Jabaha can breathe fire from his nose and mouth, and nothing is safe from a swipe of his massive talons. Considered a god by the dragonoids, his very presence invigorates the lesser Fire beings, and he has been known to turn around battles with one swoop through the enemy ranks.

Fight Fire with Fire

Two of the Fire civilization's races have hated each other for years, and now the humans and the dragonoids have amassed on the volcano fields to settle their feud once and for all. When the battle heats up, the humans might have more creatures in their army, but it's the dragonoids that are the stronger race.

BEST FIGHTER: Armored Blaster Valdios

TOUGHEST UNIT: Armored Decimator Valkaizer

GROUND SUPPORT: Brawler Zyler

the Humans
total army strength:
32,000 power

DEMOLITIONS: Explosive Dude Joe

SCOUT: Mini Titan Gett

BIG GUN: Armored Cannon Balbaro

BEST FIGHTER: Explosive Fighter Ucarn

GROUND SUPPORT: Fire Sweeper Burning Hellion

TOUGHEST UNIT: Onslaughter Triceps

tHE DRAGONOIDS
total army strength:
35,000 power

DEMOLITIONS: Blasto, Explosive Soldier

SCOUT: Bombat, General of Speed

BIG GUN: Super Explosive Volcanodon

nature civilization

The world trees touch the sky, and the balloon mushrooms suck the mana from the earth. From the highest leaves to the dirt beneath the grass and twigs, the Nature creatures live in a chaotic environment where might makes right and any creature's days could be numbered if it runs into the wrong predator.

Unlike the other civilizations, Nature has no true cities and no one race governs the others. The beast folk are the most advanced, though they are primitive compared to the neighboring civilizations.

A walk through Nature's forests and jungles can be a dangerous undertaking. If you aren't stepped on by a wandering giant, you might be squashed by an innocent horned beast looking for vegetation, struck by a random egg from an exploding colony beetle, or poisoned by a floating mushroom. Perhaps the most dangerous entities are the tree folk, which can trap victims with an aura of pleasant feelings until they're ready to eat dinner.

BALLOON MUSHROOMS

The beast folk's favorite snack also serves as a source of energy for several of Nature's creatures. The fungi grow on the dark forest floor and absorb nutrients and power from other nearby plants. As they grow, their skin sacs fill with a poisonous gas that allows them to float through the forest untouched until they're ready to expel reproductive spores.

BEAST FOLK

Believe it or not, the beast folk's most skilled warriors are as strong as dragons! As Nature's most advanced race, the beast folk forge weapons to defeat their foes in close combat, wielding swords, axes, clubs, and other hand-held weapons with superior finesse. Each beast might resemble a different animal, but they all come together as one when an enemy breaks the peace.

COLONY BEETLES

It's not easy being a beetle: As an egg, you start out inside the adult colony beetle, and when the adult explodes, you get shot out like a missile. The lucky few that embed into trees can eat the wood for food until they grow armor plating for protection. Colony beetles seldom move from one spot, preferring to eat anything in range until they are ready to explode, too.

GIANTS

Generally simpleminded and gentle, the great protectors of the forest will rip apart any being that threatens their home. The largest of Nature's creatures have thick, armorlike skin, three eyes, and horns on their shoulders. Their immense muscles withstand the heavy gravity in Nature's realm and give them the strength to move forcefully outside the forest perimeter.

GIANT INSECTS

Near the top of Nature's food chain, the meat-eating giant insects will go after any creature smaller than themselves, and that's most of the forest when you consider some of the insects reach 10 feet in diameter. Some of these predators can fly, and all of them will crunch away with mandibles and pinchers until the victim stops moving . . . permanently.

HORNED BEASTS

Just because a large beast could take you down doesn't mean that it will. Most horned beasts are quiet and peaceful. The plant-eaters live in herds, and their biggest weapon is to attack together in a massive stampede. If a single horned beast gets into danger, it will use its bulky frame, nasty horns, or pure speed to escape destruction.

MYSTERY TOTEMS

Few know that mystery totems are actually possessed by the spirits of Nature's world trees. When an enemy approaches, these hovering guards begin to chant. The low melodic voice travels through the forest and draws all the other mystery totems to the point of attack, where they combine their size and power to overwhelm any foe.

TREE FOLK

Most of Nature's creatures confront you with physical strength — the tree folk use their minds. These highly intelligent plants can project their emotions into an enemy's brain, making it feel fear, sorrow, or even happiness. Before a creature knows what happened, it is under the spell of the tree folk, which is nearly impossible to break.

LEGENDS OF NATURE

RAGING DASH-HORN

In the Nature civilization's time of greatest peril, Raging Dash-Horn answered the call of battle with a desperate cry of its own. During the Ancient War, when the treacherous Darkness creatures attacked Nature's forests, Raging Dash-Horn stood its ground while the other beasts fled, and it let loose a howl that shook everyone out of their panic and unified them once again. Together, the Raging Dash-Horn and its fellow Nature creatures took back the forest.

The Raging Dash-Horn might be the most vicious defender the forests have ever known. With enormous muscles and the power to build up mana from the trees around it, the Dash-Horn can spread this raw energy to other Nature creatures, or beat its foe through sheer strength.

It's also thought that the Raging Dash-Horn was blessed by the gods. Fossil evidence tracing the Dash-Horn has shown an impressive evolution — in less than a thousand years, it has advanced from the size of a small mouse to the massive, full-grown beast of today!

4

Silver Fist
BEAST FOLK

CREATURE

illus. Sansyu

• Power attacker +2000 *(While attacking, this creature gets +2000 power.)*

"Is one life too high a price to pay to save an entire forest?"

3000+

©2004 Wizards of the Coast/
Shogakukan/Mitsui-Kids ◆ 54/55

The giant insects all died under the massive Darkness invasion. At the outset of the Ancient War, the worms of the Darkness civilization wiped out the insects before Silver Fist and his beast folk could react in time. As the Darkness invaders fed on the corpses and bred a greater plague of ravaging worms, Silver Fist gathered the Silver Hair tribe and met the horde head–on. A short sword in hand, the legendary leader swung his tree-trunk-sized arms back and forth and cut through the worms. Silver Fist and the other beast folk tribes slew millions of Darkness worms on the battlefield and stopped that thrust of the invasion.

Today, Silver Fist is recognized as one of the most spiritual creatures living in the forest. He believes that the Light beings are gods, and has helped to forge an alliance between the two civilizations. On many occasions, he has climbed the stairways carved into their world trees, ascending the impossible heights to commune with his gods.

mean green

It's a jungle out there, and of all the civilizations, Nature knows the struggles of the Earth best. The forest's world trees produce so much mana that they have increased the gravity around the Nature villages more than anywhere else in the world. To resist this super-gravity, Nature's creatures have developed huge muscles and tend to grow up on the beefier side. Just look at this sample of Nature's habitat, from the smallest mushroom to the tallest giant.

GIANT INSECTS

Traveling in large groups, these meat-eating insects enjoy attacking the plant-eaters or any easy prey they can get their mandibles on.

TREE FOLK

Don't be fooled by their bark and roots — these trees can outthink opponents that aren't aware of their mental abilities.

BEAST FOLK

Small compared to other Nature creatures, the beasts make up for it with primitive weapons that can slash the odds against them in half.

BALLOON MUSHROOMS

They are found on the jungle floor, and mana is gained from munching on these mushrooms. Just don't eat the poisonous ones!

Rumbling Terahorn
HORNED BEAST

5

CREATURE

• When you put this creature into the battle zone, search your deck. You may take a creature from your deck, show that creature to your opponent, and put it into your hand. Then shuffle your deck.

3000

Storm Shell
COLONY BEETLE

7

CREATURE

• When you put this creature into the battle zone, your opponent chooses 1 of his creatures in the battle zone and puts it into his mana zone.

A Colony Beetle's spawning is a virtual nightmare. It covers the earth with a hail of its bullet-like eggs.

2000

(Ilus. Lonely)
©2004 Wizards of the Coast/ Shogakukan/Mitsui-Kids ★ 106/110

Dawn Giant
GIANT

7

CREATURE

(Ilus. Hideaki Takamura)

• This creature can't attack creatures.
• **Double breaker** *(This creature breaks 2 shields.)*

That's not the sound of an earthquake. That's just the Dawn Giants snoring.

11000

©2004 Wizards of the Coast/ Shogakukan/Mitsui-Kids ★ 46/55

HORNED BEASTS
They look mean and ferocious, but they're actually plant-eaters. Usually calm, they will fight back if annoyed enough.

COLONY BEETLES
These supersized beetles eat at the source of Nature's mana, the world trees. They grow so fat from overeating that a few of them have been known to explode!

GIANTS
The protectors of the forest stir only in times of great need, and once they awaken, they won't sleep until the battle is won.

3 Adomis, the Oracle
LIGHT BRINGER

CREATURE

- Instead of having this creature attack, you may tap it to use its ⊤ ability.
- ⊤ Choose a shield and look at it. Then put it back where it was.

"Aw, man—I got a speck of asteroid in my eye."

2000

5 Arc Bine, the Astounding
GUARDIAN

EVOLUTION CREATURE

- Evolution—Put one of your Guardians.
- Each of your light creatures may tap instead of attacking to use this creature's ⊤ ability.
- ⊤ Choose one of your opponent's creatures in the battle zone and tap it.

"Dragonish-like explosions! Then this is their lucky day!"

5000

2 Ballas, Vizier of Electrons
INITIATE

CREATURE

For the first time since before the Megapocalypse, the forces of Light launched a full-fledged invasion of the planet surface. The Fire troops had no choice but to retreat.

2000

4 Bonds of Justice

SPELL

- **Shield trigger** (When this spell is put into your hand from your shield zone, you may cast it immediately for no cost.)
- Tap all creatures in the battle zone that don't have "blocker."

"Need a lift?"
—Kaneslil, the Explorer

5 Chekicul, Vizier of Endurance
INITIATE

CREATURE

- **Blocker**
- Whenever this creature blocks, no battle happens. (Both creatures stay tapped.)
- This creature can't attack.

"If you don't chill out, I'll start an ice age and make you chill out!"

1000

5 Chen Treg, Vizier of Blades
INITIATE

CREATURE

- Instead of having this creature attack, you may tap it to use its ⊤ ability.
- ⊤ Choose one of your opponent's creatures in the battle zone and tap it.

Its blade, forged in the heat of stars, can penetrate any armor.

2000

4 Cosmogold, Spectral Knight
RAINBOW PHANTOM

CREATURE

- Instead of having this creature attack, you may tap it to use its ⊤ ability.
- ⊤ Return a spell from your mana zone to your hand.

He glows with the reflection of a million stars.

3000

6 Craze Valkyrie, the Drastic
INITIATE

EVOLUTION CREATURE

- Evolution—Put one of your Initiates.
- When you put this creature into the battle zone, choose up to 2 of your opponent's creatures in the battle zone and tap them.
- **Double breaker** (This creature breaks 2 shields.)

"Time to get Drastic!"

7500

6 Dava Torey, Seeker of Clouds
MECHA THUNDER

CREATURE

- During your opponent's turn, if this creature would be discarded from your hand, put it into the battle zone instead.

"I refuse to be forgotten."

5500

6 Forbos, Sanctum Guardian Q
SURVIVOR / GUARDIAN

CREATURE

- **Survivor** (Each of your Survivors has this creature's ability.)
- ⊤ When you put this creature into the battle zone, search your deck. You may take a spell from your deck, show that spell to your opponent, and put it into your hand. Then shuffle your deck.

4000

5 Gariel, Elemental of Sunbeams
ANGEL COMMAND

CREATURE

- You can summon this creature only if you have cast a spell this turn.
- **Double breaker** (This creature breaks 2 shields.)

Elementals can't stand being on the ground instead of in the sky. So when they start a war, they make sure it ends quickly.

7500

13 Invincible Aura

SPELL

- Add up to 3 cards from the top of your deck to your shields face down.

The Fire army has enough firepower to lay waste to a planet—but even that isn't enough to bring down the wall of Light.

Kanesill, the Explorer
3 — GLADIATOR
(Illus. Akifumi Yamamoto)

Blocker *(Whenever an opponent's creature attacks, you may tap this creature to stop the attack. Then the 2 creatures battle.)*
- This creature can't attack players.

The Gladiators' only job is to study the science of war. They like their job.

4000

©2005 Wizards of the Coast/
Shogakukan/Mitsui-Kids ● 20/110

Laveil, Seeker of Catastrophe
8 — MECHA THUNDER
(Illus. Masaki Hirooka)

Blocker *(Whenever an opponent's creature attacks, you may tap this creature to stop the attack. Then the 2 creatures battle.)*
- At the end of each of your turns, you may untap this creature.
- **Double breaker** *(This creature breaks 2 shields.)*

8500

©2005 Wizards of the Coast/
Shogakukan/Mitsui-Kids ● 32/110

Lightning Grass
3 — STARLIGHT TREE
(Illus. Akira Hamada)

CREATURE

The StarLight Trees' typical diet consists of moonbeams, lightning, and wisps of clouds. But they're just as happy eating the burning wreckage of broken Armorloids.

3000

©2005 Wizards of the Coast/
Shogakukan/Mitsui-Kids ● 28/110

Lu Gila, Silver Rift Guardian
5 — GUARDIAN
(Illus. Takeshi Nano)

Blocker *(Whenever an opponent's creature attacks, you may tap this creature to stop the attack. Then the 2 creatures battle.)*
- Evolution creatures are put into the battle zone tapped.
- This creature can't attack players.

4000

©2005 Wizards of the Coast/
Shogakukan/Mitsui-Kids ● 8/110

Moontear, Spectral Knight
2 — RAINBOW PHANTOM
(Illus. Tsuchika Obata)

- You can summon this creature only if you have cast a spell this turn.

All who see his sword undergo a change of heart. All who feel his sword undergo a change of intestines.

3500

©2005 Wizards of the Coast/
Shogakukan/Mitsui-Kids ● 29/110

Protective Force
1
(Illus. Kouji)

SPELL

Shield trigger *(When this spell is put into your hand from your shield zone, you may cast it immediately for no cost.)*
- One of your creatures in the battle zone that has "blocker" gets +4000 power until the end of the turn.

1

©2005 Wizards of the Coast/
Shogakukan/Mitsui-Kids ● 16/110

Rain of Arrows
2
(Illus. Katsuhiko Koyd)

SPELL

- Look at your opponent's hand. He discards all darkness spells from it.

*"Today's weather report calls for sunshine, with an 80 percent chance of kicking your butt."
—Laveil, Seeker of Catastrophe*

©2005 Wizards of the Coast/
Shogakukan/Mitsui-Kids ● 35/110

Razorpine Tree
5 — STARLIGHT TREE
(Illus. Toru Terasaka)

CREATURE

- This creature gets +2000 power for each shield you have.

It looks harmless . . . until it starts shooting its steel-piercing needles at you.

1000+

©2005 Wizards of the Coast/
Shogakukan/Mitsui-Kids ● 34/110

Sphere of Wonder
4
(Illus. Yuichi Kai)

SPELL

- If your opponent has more shields than you do, add the top card of your deck to your shields face down.

*"It's immune to swords, lasers, flames, cannonballs, acid, missiles, bottlerockets, ray guns, bee stings, paper cuts, little wooden sticks . . ."
—Telitol, the Explorer*

©2005 Wizards of the Coast/
Shogakukan/Mitsui-Kids ● 20/110

Telitol, the Explorer
4 — GLADIATOR
(Illus. Aozi Genji)

Blocker
- When you put this creature into the battle zone, you may look at your shields. Then put them back where they were.
- This creature can't attack players.

"Wherever I go, daylight follows."

3000

©2005 Wizards of the Coast/
Shogakukan/Mitsui-Kids ● 26/110

Vess, the Oracle
1 — LIGHT BRINGER
(Illus. Koei Baguwawa)

Blocker *(Whenever an opponent's creature attacks, you may tap this creature to stop the attack. Then the 2 creatures battle.)*
- This creature can't attack players.

The glow surrounding an Oracle's body is created by the songs of the Elementals.

2000

©2005 Wizards of the Coast/
Shogakukan/Mitsui-Kids ● 28/110

Vuluk, the Oracle
1 — LIGHT BRINGER
(Illus. Suzuya)

- You can summon this creature only if you have cast a spell this turn.

"As an Oracle, I have the power to see the future. But my lottery numbers still never get picked!"

2500

©2005 Wizards of the Coast/
Shogakukan/Mitsui-Kids ● 35/110

Aeropica
SEA HACKER
7

CREATURE

- Instead of having this creature attack, you may tap it to use its 🔵 ability.
- 🔵 Choose a creature in the battle zone and return it to its owner's hand.

"I'm the garbage collector. You're the garbage."

4000

Aqua Rider
LIQUID PEOPLE
4

CREATURE

- Whenever your opponent summons a creature or casts a spell, this creature gets "blocker" until the end of the turn. (Whenever an opponent's creature attacks, you may tap a creature that has "blocker" to stop the attack. Then the 2 creatures battle.)

"Hey, pal—watch where you stick that fin!"

2000

Crystal Jouster
LIQUID PEOPLE
7

EVOLUTION CREATURE

- Evolution—Put on one of your Liquid People.
- Double breaker (This creature breaks 2 shields.)
- When this creature would be destroyed, return it to your hand instead.

An infinite number of warriors in one.

7000

Energy Stream
3

SPELL

- Draw 2 cards.

"Some computer programs attack our enemies. Some defend our cities. And some—the most perfect of all—just write more computer programs." —Emeral

Fort Megacluster
CYBER CLUSTER
5

EVOLUTION CREATURE

- Evolution—Put on one of your Cyber Clusters.
- Each of your water creatures may tap instead of attacking to use this creature's 🔵 ability.
- 🔵 Draw a card.

The Cyber Lords are racing the Dragonoids to be the first to drill to the planet's core.

5000

Hazard Crawler
EARTH EATER
5

CREATURE

- 🔵 Blocker (Whenever an opponent's creature attacks, you may tap this creature to stop the attack.)
- This creature can't attack.

All life came from the sea. Now the sea's coming to take it back.

8000

Invincible Technology
13

SPELL

- Search your deck. You may take any number of cards from your deck, show those cards to your opponent, and put them into your hand. Then shuffle your deck.

The Acashic Database holds the secrets of the universe. After centuries of searching, the Cyber Lords have at last found a clue to deciphering it.

King Triumphant
LEVIATHAN
8

CREATURE

- Whenever your opponent summons a creature or casts a spell, this creature gets "blocker" until the end of the turn. (Whenever an opponent's creature attacks, you may tap a creature that has "blocker" to stop the attack. Then the 2 creatures battle.)
- Double breaker (This creature breaks 2 shields.)

7000

Kyuroro
CYBER LORD
6

CREATURE

- Whenever an opponent's creature would break a shield, you choose the shield instead of your opponent.

"These tubes connect me to everything. That fat one there goes right into your brain."

2000

Madrillon Fish
GEL FISH
2

CREATURE

- 🔵 Blocker (Whenever an opponent's creature attacks, you may tap this creature to stop the attack. Then the 2 creatures battle.)
- This creature can't attack.

"I see they've loosened the definition of 'fish.'" —Cantankerous Giant

3000

Midnight Crawler
EARTH EATER
8

CREATURE

- When you put this creature into the battle zone, choose a card in your opponent's mana zone and return it to his hand.
- Double breaker (This creature breaks 2 shields.)

"If you see a pair of twinkling red stars at night, watch out—there's likely a mouth attached to them." —Fear Fang

8000

Mystic Dreamscape
4

SPELL

- 🔵 Shield trigger (When this spell is put into your hand from your shield zone, you may cast it immediately for no cost.)
- Return up to 3 cards from your mana zone to your hand.

"Don't worry! No one gets arrested for breaking the laws of nature anymore."

Neon Cluster
CYBER CLUSTER
7

(Illus. Sansyu)

CREATURE

• Instead of having this creature attack, you may tap it to use its Ⓖ ability.
Ⓖ Draw 2 cards.

"You can win more wars by thinking than you can by fighting."
—Martranmancer

4000

©2001 Wizards of the Coast® Shogakukan/Mitsui-Kids ◆ 40/110

Overload Cluster
CYBER CLUSTER
5

(Illus. Kaneyo)

CREATURE

• Whenever your opponent summons a creature or casts a spell, this creature gets "blocker" until the end of the turn. *(Whenever an opponent's creature attacks, you may tap a creature that has "blocker" to stop the attack. Then the 2 creatures battle.)*

4000

©2001 Wizards of the Coast® Shogakukan/Mitsui-Kids ◆ 41/110

Promephius Q
SURVIVOR / SEA HACKER
3

(Illus. D-Suzuki)

CREATURE

"It is my spy into the Survivor clan. They have accepted it as one of their own. And it has learned all their secrets."
—Emperor Quozilo

2000

©2001 Wizards of the Coast® Shogakukan/Mitsui-Kids ◆ 42/110

Q-tronic Hypermind
SURVIVOR
8

(Illus. Jason)

EVOLUTION CREATURE

• Evolution—Put on one of your Survivors.
• When you put this creature into the battle zone, you may draw a card for each Survivor in the battle zone.
• Double breaker *(This creature breaks 2 shields.)*

"Don't let me think too hard. It makes the world explode."

8000

©2001 Wizards of the Coast® Shogakukan/Mitsui-Kids ◆ 43/110

Raptor Fish
GEL FISH
6

(Illus. Masaki Yamamoto)

CREATURE

• When you put this creature into the battle zone, count the cards in your hand, shuffle those cards into your deck, then draw that many cards.

*"Its control chip is busted. Each time it blinks, I—"
"Its control chip is busted. Each time it blinks, I—"*
—Sopian

3000

©2001 Wizards of the Coast® Shogakukan/Mitsui-Kids ◆ 44/110

Ripple Lotus Q
SURVIVOR / CYBER VIRUS
6

(Illus. Katsuhiko Kojoh)

CREATURE

• Survivor *(Each of your Survivors has this creature's ability.)*
Ⓤ When you put this creature into the battle zone, you may choose one of your opponent's creatures in the battle zone and tap it.

Its petals wave gently in the current, tempting prey to come closer to its poisonous tendrils.

2000

©2001 Wizards of the Coast® Shogakukan/Mitsui-Kids ◆ 46/110

Shock Hurricane
5

(Illus. Naoki)

SPELL

• Return any number of your creatures from the battle zone to your hand. Then you may choose that many of your opponent's creatures in the battle zone and return them to your opponent's hand.

"I wish I had my umbrellaooooooooooooooooooo!"

©2001 Wizards of the Coast® Shogakukan/Mitsui-Kids ◆ 45/110

Sopian
CYBER LORD
4

(Illus. Katsuhiko Kojoh)

CREATURE

• Instead of having this creature attack, you may tap it to use its Ⓤ ability.
Ⓤ Choose one of your creatures in the battle zone. It can't be blocked this turn.

It doesn't just live like the Ultracomputer—it's part of the circuitry.

2000

©2001 Wizards of the Coast® Shogakukan/Mitsui-Kids ◆ 47/110

Spiral Gate
2

(Illus. Tomofumi Ogasawara)

SPELL

◆ Shield trigger *(When this spell is put into your hand from your shield zone, you may cast it immediately for no cost.)*
• Choose a creature in the battle zone and return it to its owner's hand.

©2001 Wizards of the Coast® Shogakukan/Mitsui-Kids ◆ 48/110

Steam Star
CYBER VIRUS
2

(Illus. D-Suzuki)

CREATURE

The Cyber Lords deploy them at volcanic vents on the bottom of the ocean. They monitor the superheated steam, collect it, and—when necessary—use it as a weapon.

1000

©2001 Wizards of the Coast® Shogakukan/Mitsui-Kids ◆ 49/110

Thrash Crawler
EARTH EATER
4

(Illus. Yuko Tsukamoto)

CREATURE

Ⓑ Blocker
• When you put this creature into the battle zone, return a card from your mana zone to your hand.
• This creature can't attack.

Erosion . . . with a vengeance.

5000

©2001 Wizards of the Coast® Shogakukan/Mitsui-Kids ◆ 80/110

Zepimeteus
SEA HACKER
1

(Illus. Naoki Saito)

CREATURE

Ⓑ Blocker *(Whenever an opponent's creature attacks, you may tap this creature to stop the attack. Then the 2 creatures battle.)*
• This creature can't attack.

Those used to be nuclear submarines. Now they're bathtub toys.

2000

©2001 Wizards of the Coast® Shogakukan/Mitsui-Kids ◆ 50/110

Bazooka Mutant
HEDRIAN

4 / 8000

- This creature can attack only creatures that have "blocker."
- This creature can't attack players.

The cannon is covered in slime. It runs on slime. It's fired by slime. Guess what it shoots?

Cursed Pincher
BRAIN JACKER

4 / 2000

- Blocker (Whenever an opponent's creature attacks, you may tap this creature to stop the attack. Then the 2 creatures battle.)
- Slayer (Whenever this creature battles, destroy the other creature after the battle.)
- This creature can't attack.

Daidalos, General of Fury
DEMON COMMAND

4 / 11000

- Whenever this creature attacks, destroy one of your creatures.
- Double breaker (This creature breaks 2 shields.)

"Friend or foe? Dragonoid, Gooneage, or Giant? They're all the same. They're all threats."

Death Smoke
SPELL

4

- Destroy one of your opponent's untapped creatures.

"Life is like this joke. It's very, very funny, and now it's over."
—Drax, Wicked Doll

Frost Specter, Shadow of Age
GHOST

3 / 5000

EVOLUTION CREATURE

- Evolution—Put one of your Ghosts.
- Each of your Ghosts in the battle zone has "slayer." (Whenever a creature that has "slayer" battles, destroy the other creature after the battle.)

"The young get older. The old get older. And everyone forgets my birthday."

Future Slash
SPELL

7

- Search your opponent's deck. Take up to 2 cards from his deck and put them into his graveyard. Then your opponent shuffles his deck.

"Look on the bright side. Next time a fortune-teller predicts your future, you can ask for a discount."
—Schuba, Duke of Amnesia

Gigagriff
CHIMERA

6 / 4000

- Blocker (Whenever an opponent's creature attacks, you may tap this creature to stop the attack. Then the 2 creatures battle.)
- Slayer (Whenever this creature battles, destroy the other creature after the battle.)
- This creature can't attack.

Gnarvash, Merchant of Blood
DEMON COMMAND

6 / 8000

- Double breaker (This creature breaks 2 shields.)
- At the end of each of your turns, if this is your only creature in the battle zone, destroy it.

His mother was right. His face did freeze like that.

Grave Worm Q
SURVIVOR / PARASITE WORM

5 / 3000

- Survivor (Each of your Survivors has this creature's ability.)
- When you put this creature into the battle zone, you may return a Survivor from your graveyard to your hand.

Its swimmer can unkill an unkilled thing in twenty seconds flat.

Grim Soul, Shadow of Reversal
GHOST

5 / 3000

- Instead of having this creature attack, you may tap it to use its ability.
- Return a darkness creature from your graveyard to your hand.

"Quit being dead. Your lifetime contract with Boilam hasn't expired yet."

Grinning Axe, the Monstrosity
DEVIL MASK

3 / 1000

- Slayer (Whenever this creature battles, destroy the other creature after the battle.)

"That thing looks like it's eating its own face!"
—Miel Titan Gett

Intense Evil
SPELL

3

- Shield trigger (When this spell is put into your hand from your shield zone, you may cast it immediately for no cost.)
- Destroy any number of your creatures. Then draw that many cards.

Every soul has a price—and today they're on sale!

Invincible Abyss — 13 — SPELL
(Ill. Atushi Kawasaki)

- Destroy all your opponent's creatures.

After the latest Nature victories in the Fiona Woods, Ballom decided to host peace talks at the sacred Xkalmic Crater. The stadium filled with Nature and Light representatives, but Ballom, Trox, and Daidalos never showed. As if on cue, the crater started belching toxic gas. . . .

2

Junkatz, Rabid Doll — 2 — DEATH PUPPET
CREATURE (Ill. Eiji Kaneda)

After a humiliating defeat under the hooves of the Nature hordes, Ballom started to play with Doll.

2000

Lone Tear, Shadow of Solitude — 1 — GHOST
CREATURE (Ill. Anni Geeth)

- At the end of each of your turns, if this is your only creature in the battle zone, destroy it.

It's the tollbooth operator on the highway of despair.

2000

Lupa, Poison-Tipped Doll — 2 — DEATH PUPPET
CREATURE (Ill. Yorikatu Miyoshi)

- Instead of having this creature attack, you may tap it to use its ability.
- One of your creatures in the battle zone gets "slayer" until the end of the turn. (Whenever a creature that has "slayer" battles, destroy the other creature after the battle.)

1000

Phantasmal Horror Gigazald — 5 — CHIMERA
EVOLUTION CREATURE (Ill. Nottsuo)

- Evolution—Put on one of your Chimeras.
- Each of your darkness creatures may tap instead of attacking to use this creature's ability.
- Your opponent discards a card at random from his hand.

"Pretend I'm a nightmare. You won't go so insane that way."

5000

Proclamation of Death — 4 — SPELL
(Ill. Atushi Kawasaki)

- Shield trigger (When this spell is put into your hand from your shield zone, you may cast it immediately for no cost.)
- Your opponent chooses one of his creatures in the battle zone and destroys it.

2

Schuka, Duke of Amnesia — 6 — DARK LORD
CREATURE (Ill. Daisuke Izuka)

- When this creature is destroyed, each player discards his hand.

"All the mysteries of the universe—the eternal questions of past, present, and future—pretty much boil down to this: how do you like my spiffy new cape?"

5000

Skullcutter, Swarm Leader — 4 — DEVIL MASK
CREATURE (Ill. Daisuke Izuka)

- At the end of each of your turns, if this is your only creature in the battle zone, destroy it.

"Good job, everyone! The diet is really working!"

4000

Tank Mutant — 9 — HEDRIAN
CREATURE (Ill. Akira Hamada)

- Instead of having this creature attack, you may tap it to use its ability.
- Your opponent chooses one of his creatures in the battle zone and destroys it.

"Fire the Shocktacular Zaphtonic Megaparticle Laserblaster Disraptolating Cannon! No, the other one."

6000

Tentacle Worm — 4 — PARASITE WORM
CREATURE (Ill. Kap Nolambao)

Deep in the roots of the Fiona Woods, the seeds of destruction writhe, squirm, crawl . . . and multiply.

3000

Vile Mulder, Wing of the Void — 4 — DEMON COMMAND
CREATURE (Ill. Tv Buchak)

- This creature can't attack creatures.
- Double breaker (This creature breaks 2 shields.)
- When this creature battles, destroy it after the battle.

Its heart rings for conquest. Its blood rings a dirge of doom.

7000

Zorvaz, the Bonecrusher — 5 — DEMON COMMAND
CREATURE (Ill. Nottoki Mammoto)

- Blocker (Whenever an opponent's creature attacks, you may tap this creature to stop the attack. Then the 2 creatures battle.)
- This creature can't attack.
- When this creature battles, destroy it after the battle.

8000

5 Armored Decimator Valkaizer
HERO

- Evolution—Put on one of your Humans.
- When you put this creature into the battle zone, you may destroy one of your opponent's creatures that has power 4000 or less.

"With a gun this big, how can I miss?"

5000

5 Armored Scout Gestuchar
ARMORLOID

- While you have no other fire creatures in the battle zone, this creature has "power attacker +3000" and "double breaker." (A creature that has "power attacker +3000" and "double breaker" gets +3000 power while attacking and breaks 2 shields.)

An Armorloid's armor has two stages: Ironsome warrior and scrap metal.

4000+

4 Automated Weaponmaster Machac
ARMORLOID

- This creature attacks each turn if able.

"Stupid Light creatures—its spheres and birds and energy clouds. How can I blow their heads off if they don't have any?"

4000

5 Badlands Lizard
DUNE GECKO

- Power attacker +3000 (While attacking, this creature gets +3000 power.)
- Whenever this creature becomes blocked, no battle happens. (Both creatures stay tapped.)

"I traded in my sportutility Gecko for a stretch Geckousine."
—Artisan Picora

3000+

8 Bazagazeal Dragon
ARMORED DRAGON

- Speed attacker (This creature doesn't get summoning sickness.)
- This creature can attack untapped creatures.
- Double breaker (This creature breaks 2 shields.)
- At the end of your turn, return this creature to your hand.

8000

7 Bolmeteus Steel Dragon
ARMORED DRAGON

- Double breaker (This creature breaks 2 shields.)
- Whenever this creature would break a shield, your opponent puts that shield into his graveyard instead.

Part robot. Part Dragon. All trouble.

7000

2 Choya, the Unbeeding
HUMAN

- Power attacker +1000 (While attacking, this creature gets +1000 power.)
- Whenever this creature becomes blocked, no battle happens. (Both creatures stay tapped.)

"Dude, check this out." SPROING!

1000+

3 Cocco Lupia
FIRE BIRD

- Your creatures that have Dragon in their race each cost 2 less to summon. (Dragonoids don't count.) They can't cost less than 2.

Each Fire Bird is given one Dragon egg to take care of. After the Dragon hatches, the Fire Bird is a lifetime.

1000

1 Comet Missile

- Shield trigger (When this spell is put into your hand from your shield zone, you may cast it immediately for no cost.)
- Destroy one of your opponent's creatures that has "blocker" and power 6000 or less.

"The masters of subtlety are at it again."
—Craze Valkyrie, the Drastic

4 Crisis Boulder

- Shield trigger (When this spell is put into your hand from your shield zone, you may cast it immediately for no cost.)
- Your opponent chooses one of his creatures in the battle zone or a card in his mana zone and puts it into his graveyard.

3 Cutthroat Skyterror
ARMORED WYVERN

- Speed attacker (This creature doesn't get summoning sickness.)
- This creature can't attack players.
- At the end of your turn, return this creature to your hand.

5000

13 Invincible Cataclysm

- Choose up to 3 of your opponent's shields and put them into his graveyard.

The brutal forces of Light leveled the capital of the Fire realm. But deep in the mountains, the Fire doomsday weapon waits to take revenge.

Lava Walker Executo
DRAGONOID

- Evolution—Put on one of your Dragonoids.
- Each of your fire creatures can tap instead of attacking to use that creature's 🔆 ability.
- 🔆 One of your fire creatures in the battle zone gets +3000 power until the end of the turn.

"Ouch! Ouch! Hot hot hot!"

4 / 5000

Legionnaire Lizard
DUNE GECKO

- Speed attacker (This creature doesn't get summoning sickness.)
- Instead of having this creature attack, you may tap it to use its 🔆 ability.
- 🔆 One of your creatures in the battle zone gets "speed attacker" until the end of the turn.

6 / 4000

Migasa, Adept of Chaos
HUMAN

- Instead of having this creature attack, you may tap it to use its 🔆 ability.
- 🔆 One of your creatures in the battle zone gets "double breaker" until the end of the turn. (A creature that has "double breaker" breaks 2 shields.)

3 / 2000

Phantom Dragon's Flame

- 🔆 Shield trigger (When this spell is put into your hand from your shield zone, you may cast it immediately for no cost.)
- Destroy one of your opponent's creatures that has power 2000 or less.

"Would you prefer a real Dragon?"

3

Picora's Wrench
MECHA PARTS

The Machine Eaters are a race of invention and mechanics. One day, bored out of their minds, they decided it would be funny to grant life to their tools—and the XenoParts were born.

2 / 2000

Pyrofighter Magnus
DRAGONOID

- Speed attacker (This creature doesn't get summoning sickness.)
- At the end of your turn, return this creature to your hand.

At maximum speed, he reaches escape velocity and teleports to a whole new dimension . . . but which one?

3 / 3000

Q-tronic Gargantua
SURVIVOR

- Evolution—Put on one of your Survivors.
- Crew breaker—Survivor (This creature breaks one more shield for each of your other Survivors in the battle zone.)

A disaster nearly doomed the Survivors. Now disasters merely fuel their fury.

6 / 9000

Rikabu's Screwdriver
XENOPARTS

- Instead of having this creature attack, you may tap it to use its 🔆 ability.
- 🔆 Destroy one of your opponent's creatures that has "blocker."

It's good at putting things together. It's better at taking things apart.

2 / 1000

Rumblesaur Q
SURVIVOR / ROCK BEAST

- Survivor (Each of your Survivors has this creature's 🔆 ability.)
- Speed attacker (This creature doesn't get summoning sickness.)

"You'd run fast too, if you were on fire."

6 / 3000

Spastic Missile

- Destroy one of your opponent's creatures that has power 3000 or less.

"Hee hee! The missiles are having as much fun as I am!"
—Rikabu, the Dismantler

3

Torchclencher
DRAGONOID

- While you have at least one other fire creature in the battle zone, this creature has "Power attacker +3000 (While attacking, this creature gets +3000 power)."

When the Elementals attacked, no one in the Fire realm joined the army. They were all already in it.

3 / 2000+

Valiant Warrior Exorious
ARMORLOID

- This creature can attack untapped creatures.
- Power attacker +3000 (While attacking, this creature gets +3000 power.)

"If you ever want to find me, just look between the explosion."

6 / 4000+

6 — Bliss Totem, Avatar of Luck
MYSTERY TOTEM

CREATURE
• Instead of having this creature attack, you may tap it to use its ⓖ ability.
ⓖ Put up to 3 cards from your graveyard into your mana zone.

"Someone call a doctor—I've got bongo fever!"

5000

7 — Cantankerous Giant
GIANT

CREATURE
• Double breaker (This creature breaks 2 shields.)

"I've been tracking an immense creature across the continent by following its huge footprints. One thing puzzles me, though—since when do footprints have thumbs?"
—Feather Horn, the Tracker

8000

3 — Carrier Shell
COLONY BEETLE

CREATURE
• Power attacker +3000 (While attacking, this creature gets +3000 power.)

The rocky plains where Colony Beetles lay their eggs eventually became fertile fields covered in grass and flowers.

2000+

4 — Charmilia, the Enticer
SNOW FAERIE

CREATURE
• Instead of having this creature attack, you may tap it to use its ⓖ ability.
ⓖ Search your deck. You may take a creature from your deck, show that creature to your opponent, and put it into your hand. Then shuffle your deck.

"Hmm. Flurry or blizzard?"

3000

5 — Cliffcrush Giant
GIANT

CREATURE
• While you have any other untapped creatures in the battle zone, this creature can't attack.
• Double breaker (This creature breaks 2 shields.)

The last time the only thing untapped on the mountain was the top of the mountain.

7000

6 — Clobber Totem
MYSTERY TOTEM

CREATURE
• Power attacker +2000 (While attacking, this creature gets +2000 power.)
• This creature can't be blocked by any creature that has power 5000 or less.
• Double breaker (This creature breaks 2 shields.)

4000+

3 — Dimension Gate

SPELL
◆ Shield trigger (When this spell is put into your hand from your shield zone, you may cast it immediately for no cost.)
• Search your deck. You may take a creature from your deck, show that creature to your opponent, and put it into your hand. Then shuffle your deck.

6 — Factory Shell Q
SURVIVOR / COLONY BEETLE

CREATURE
• Survivor (Each of your Survivors has this creature's ⓖ ability.)
ⓖ When you put this creature into the battle zone, search your deck. You may take a Survivor from your deck, show that Survivor to your opponent, and put it into your hand. Then shuffle your deck.

2000

2 — Faerie Life

SPELL
◆ Shield trigger (When this spell is put into your hand from your shield zone, you may cast it immediately for no cost.)
• Put the top card of your deck into your mana zone.

4 — Feather Horn, the Tracker
HORNED BEAST

CREATURE

"If it's true that you are what you eat, it looks like somebody's been chowing down on way too many flamingos."
—Kyvorra

4000

5 — Forbidding Totem
MYSTERY TOTEM

CREATURE
• Your opponent's attacking creatures attack Mystery Totems if able.

The personality of an avatar is a reflection of the concept it represents. For example, the avatar of war is straightforward and difficult to control.

4000

2 — Garabon, the Glider
SNOW FAERIE

CREATURE
• Power attacker +2000 (While attacking, this creature gets +2000 power.)

"Toooonight! Who's up for a snowball fight?"

1000+

3 · **Illusory Berry**
TREE FOLK
CREATURE

"We rise from the shadow of the Flame Woods. We rise to exact our well-earned revenge. We rise to—oh, man, did Slappin's head pop again? Great. Way to ruin my dramatic speech, Slappin."

3000

4 · **Innocent Hunter, Blade of All**
BEAST FOLK
CREATURE

- You can put an evolution creature of any race on this creature.

His soul is so pure that anywhere he wanders accepts him as a native son. His infinite destinies lie just over the horizon.

1000

13 · **Invincible Unity**
SPELL

- Each of your creatures in the battle zone gets +8000 power and "triple breaker" until the end of the turn. *(A creature that has "triple breaker" breaks 3 shields.)*

The roots of the World Tree reach into the hearts of all who cherish life.

5 · **Living Citadel Vosh**
COLONY BEETLE
EVOLUTION CREATURE

- Evolution—Put on one of your Colony Beetles.
- Each of your nature creatures may tap instead of attacking to use this creature's ☉ ability.
- ☉ Put the top card of your deck into your mana zone.

A faithful imitation of the World Tree.

5000

3 · **Mighty Bandit, Ace of Thieves**
BEAST FOLK
CREATURE

- Instead of having this creature attack, you may tap it to use its ☉ ability.
- ☉ One of your creatures in the battle zone gets +5000 power until the end of the turn.

"Get real. I've never bucked a swash in my life."

2000

3 · **Mystic Treasure Chest**
SPELL

- Search your deck. You may take a non-nature card from your deck and put it into your mana zone. Then shuffle your deck.

Mighty Bandit didn't earn his name by robbing piggy banks. Well, not just piggy banks.

3 · **Pangaea's Will**
SPELL

- Shield trigger *(When this spell is put into your hand from your shield zone, you may cast it immediately for no cost.)*
- Choose one of your opponent's evolution creatures in the battle zone and put the top card of that creature into your opponent's mana zone.

4 · **Paradise Horn**
HORNED BEAST
CREATURE

- Power attacker +2000 *(While attacking, this creature gets +2000 power.)*

Few places on the planet still know the joy of absolute peace. Paradise Horn makes sure this is one of them.

3000+

2 · **Slumber Shell**
COLONY BEETLE
CREATURE

It hasn't moved from that spot for a hundred years. Based on the normal lifespan of a Colony Beetle, it's taking a quick nap.

2000

7 · **Splinterclaw Wasp**
GIANT INSECT
CREATURE

- Power attacker +3000 *(While attacking, this creature gets +3000 power.)*
- Double breaker *(This creature breaks 2 shields.)*
- Whenever this creature becomes blocked, it breaks one of your opponent's shields.

"Buzz off."

4000+

3 · **Trench Scarab**
GIANT INSECT
CREATURE

- This creature can't attack players.
- Power attacker +4000 *(While attacking, this creature gets +4000 power.)*

Since their sharp blades are dangerous even to one another, these insects tend to live alone.

4000+

6 · **Ultra Mantis, Scourge of Fate**
GIANT INSECT
EVOLUTION CREATURE

- Evolution—Put on one of your Giant Insects.
- This creature can't be blocked by any creature that has power 8000 or less.
- Double breaker *(This creature breaks 2 shields.)*

It doesn't need a weapon—it is a weapon.

9000

Bex, the Oracle
3
LIGHT BRINGER

Illus. Santyo

CREATURE

• While you have no shields, this creature has "Blocker (Whenever an opponent's creature attacks, you may tap this creature to stop the attack. Then the 2 creatures battle.)"

"Two . . . four . . . three . . . two . . ."

2500

Gandar, Seeker of Explosions
7
MECHA THUNDER

Illus. Katsuya

CREATURE

• Double breaker (This creature breaks 2 shields.)
• Instead of having this creature attack, you may tap it to use its ⚡ ability.
• ⚡ At the end of the turn, untap all your light creatures.

He has a short fuse.

8500

Geoshine, Spectral Knight
5
RAINBOW PHANTOM

Illus. Eiji Kaneda

CREATURE

• Whenever this creature attacks, you may choose a darkness or fire creature in the battle zone and tap it. (First choose what this creature is attacking. Then choose a creature to tap.)

"A broken sword becomes an even sharper weapon."

4000

Justice Jamming
3

Illus. Koei

SPELL

• Tap all darkness creatures in the battle zone, or tap all fire creatures in the battle zone.

Sky Crusher's army couldn't decide which was worse—when the forbidding stone tablets rose up, or when the forbidding stone tablets fell over.

Kizar Basiku, the Outrageous
5
INITIATE

Illus. Mitki

⚡ EVOLUTION CREATURE

• ☐ Blocker (Whenever an opponent's creature attacks, you may tap this creature to stop the attack. Then the 2 creatures battle.)
• Evolution—Put on one of your Initiates.
• Fire stealth (This creature can't be blocked while your opponent has any fire cards in his mana zone.)
• Double breaker (This creature breaks 2 shields.)

8500

Lightning Charger
4

Illus. Itoe Koji

SPELL

• Choose one of your opponent's creatures in the battle zone and tap it.
• Charger (After you cast this spell, put it into your mana zone instead of your graveyard.)

"The more they squirm, the more it tickles."
—Mele, Vizier of Lightning

10/55

Miracle Portal
4

Illus. Kobashibo Koishi

SPELL

• Choose one of your creatures in the battle zone. This turn, it can't be blocked and you ignore any effects that would prevent that creature from attacking your opponent. (For example, ignore summoning sickness and card effects that say "This creature can't attack" or "This creature can't attack players." Your creatures can't attack creatures this way.)

11/55

Pulsar Tree
5
STARLIGHT TREE

Illus. Naoki Saito

CREATURE

• When one of your shields would be broken, you may destroy this creature instead.

They are the generators that power the Light civilization's floating fortresses. But did they grow into the cities, or did the cities grow out of them?

1000

Rodi Gale, Night Guardian
4
GUARDIAN

Illus. Shimotsky

CREATURE

• Darkness stealth (This creature can't be blocked while your opponent has any darkness cards in his mana zone.)

The wounds of war run deep . . . and are full of pus.

3500

Rom, Vizier of Tendrils
4
INITIATE

Illus. Ken Sugimura

CREATURE

• When you put this creature into the battle zone, you may choose one of your opponent's creatures in the battle zone and tap it.

"Vizier of Tendrils, arise. Your grip is the beacon that leads the way."
—Hanusa, Radiance Elemental

2000

Rondobil, the Explorer
6
GLADIATOR

Illus. Akku Kaneda

CREATURE

• Instead of having this creature attack, you may tap it to use its ⚡ ability.
• ⚡ Add one of your creatures from the battle zone to your shields face down.

"No fair! They flew in and sucked up all our lava! How can I take a bath now?"
—Artisan Picora

5000

Siri, Glory Elemental
6
ANGEL COMMAND

Illus. Bettun

CREATURE

• Double breaker (This creature breaks 2 shields.)
• While you have no shields, this creature has "blocker" and "At the end of each of your turns, you may untap this creature."

"I'm not building a slaughter machine . . . I am a weather machine!"

7000

Aqua Agent
LIQUID PEOPLE
6
CREATURE
- Water stealth (This creature can't be blocked while your opponent has any water cards in his mana zone.)
- When this creature would be destroyed, you may return it to your hand instead.

Atop the towers of Light, the rogue spy was given the target of his next mission: home.
2000

Aqua Fencer
LIQUID PEOPLE
7
CREATURE
- Instead of having this creature attack, you may tap it to use its ability.
  Choose a card in your opponent's mana zone and return it his hand.

His opponents are up beside themselves in anger.
3000

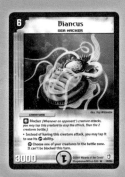

Biancus
SEA HACKER
6
CREATURE
- Blocker (Whenever an opponent's creature attacks, you may tap this creature to stop the attack. Then the 2 creatures battle.)
- Instead of having this creature attack, you may tap it to use its ability.
  Choose one of your creatures in the battle zone. It can't be blocked this turn.
3000

Cetibols
SEA HACKER
3
CREATURE
- When this creature is destroyed, you may draw a card.

"What's that smell?" —Mighty Bandit
2000

Cosmic Nebula
CYBER VIRUS
5
EVOLUTION CREATURE
- Evolution—Put on one of your Cyber Viruses.
- Whenever you draw the card at the start of your turn, you may draw an extra card.

"Time is circular. Yesterday is tomorrow. Last month is a week from Thursday. I have a headache." —Shira
3000

Curious Eye
CYBER VIRUS
3
CREATURE
- Whenever this creature attacks, you may look at one of your opponent's shields. Then put it back where it was.

"The spies I send into the Darkness realm get caught when their teeth chatter in fear. I think I've solved the problem." —Kyurius
1000

Garatyano
SEA HACKER
4
CREATURE
- Instead of having this creature attack, you may tap it to use its ability.
  Look at the top 3 cards of your deck. Then put them back in any order.

To cope with their unexpected setbacks, the Cyber Lords began recruiting and modifying even the most resistant inhabitants of the sea.
2000

King Benthos
LEVIATHAN
8
CREATURE
- Double breaker (This creature breaks 2 shields.)
- Instead of having this creature attack, you may tap it to use its ability.
  Each of your water creatures gets "This creature can't be blocked" until the end of the turn.
6000

Riptide Charger
SPELL
5
- Choose a creature in the battle zone and return it to its owner's hand.
- Charger (After you cast this spell, put it into your mana zone instead of your graveyard.)

"Congratulations! You've won an all-expenses-paid trip to Anywhere Else. Thanks for playing!" —Corila

Splash Zebrafish
GEL FISH
4
CREATURE
- When you put this creature into the battle zone, return a card from your mana zone to your hand.
- This creature can't be blocked.

"That's the only thing I've ever seen come out of a whirlpool." —Jara, Visier of Bullets
3000

Titanium Cluster
CYBER CLUSTER
4
CREATURE
- Blocker (Whenever an opponent's creature attacks, you may tap this creature to stop the attack. Then the 2 creatures battle.)
- This creature can't be attacked.
- This creature can't attack.

Deep beneath the waves, sensational, the program that would betray its masters began to run.
4000

Trenchdive Shark
GEL FISH
7
CREATURE
- When you put this creature into the battle zone, you may add up to 2 cards from your hand to your shields face down. If you do, choose the same number of your shields and put them into your hand. You can't use the "shield trigger" ability of those shields.

"Better . . . But let's add another eye." —Emeral
5000

6 Battleship Mutant
HEDRIAN

- Instead of having this creature attack, you may tap it to use its ⓒ ability.
- ⓒ Until the end of the turn, each of your darkness creatures in the battle zone gets +4000 power and "double breaker." Whenever any of those creatures battles this turn, destroy it after the battle.

5000+

8 Crath Lade, Merciless King
DARK LORD

- Instead of having this creature attack, you may tap it to use its ⓒ ability.
- ⓒ Your opponent discards 2 cards at random from his hand.

"Mortals are my crops. Their time is my harvest."

4000

4 Dream Pirate, Shadow of Theft
GHOST

- When this creature would be destroyed, you may return it to your hand instead. If you do, put a card from your hand into your graveyard.

"Arexi, me mateys, and check out me new pirate dictionary! Arrrr. Yo ho ho. Hmm, it's pretty short. Arrrr!"

3000

3 Gezary, Undercover Doll
DEATH PUPPET

- Nature stealth (This creature can't be blocked while your opponent has any nature cards in his mana zone.)

"The strings that make it dance come from deep within the ground. Wait . . . that doesn't make any sense. . . ."
—Tangle Fist

2000

5 Gigabuster
CHIMERA

- ⬛ Blocker (Whenever an opponent's creature attacks, you may tap this creature to stop the attack. Then the 2 creatures battle.)
- When you put this creature into the battle zone, choose one of your shields and put it into your hand. You can't use the "shield trigger" ability of that shield.
- This creature can't attack.

5000

5 Hopeless Vortex
SPELL

- Destroy one of your opponent's creatures.

"How do you know you won't like excruciating pain? Have you ever tried it?"
—Crath Lade, Merciless King

5 Phantasmal Horror Gigazabal
CHIMERA

- Evolution—Put on one of your Chimeras.
- Light stealth (This creature can't be blocked while your opponent has any light cards in his mana zone.)
- Double breaker (This creature breaks 2 shields.)

One moment, a gleaming city. The next moment, ash.

9000

2 Propeller Mutant
HEDRIAN

- When this creature is destroyed, your opponent discards a card at random from his hand.

"Being a plane is cool, but my real dream is to be a pile of smoldering wreckage!"

1000

3 Scalpel Spider
BRAIN JACKER

- Whenever this creature is attacked, it gets "slayer" until the end of the turn. (Whenever a creature that has "slayer" battles, destroy the other creature after the battle.)

Finding a scalpel spider is easy. Just search the web.

2000

4 Three-Faced Ashura Fang
DEVIL MASK

- When you put this creature into the battle zone, choose one of your shields and put it into your hand. You can't use the "shield trigger" ability of that shield.

It'll never turn its back on you. It can't.

4000

4 Vacuum Gel
SPELL

- ⬛ Shield trigger (When this spell is put into your hand from your shield zone, you may cast it immediately for no cost.)
- Destroy one of your opponent's untapped light or untapped nature creatures.

"I hope you're not allergic to slime. Nah, I'm just kidding."
—Mongrel Man

3 Venom Charger
SPELL

- One of your creatures in the battle zone gets "slayer" until the end of the turn. (Whenever a creature that has "slayer" battles, destroy the other creature after the battle.)
- Charger (After you cast this spell, put it into your mana zone instead of your graveyard.)

THUNDERCHARGE OF ULTRA DESTRUCTION (FIRE)

7 Apocalypse Vise

- Destroy any number of your opponent's creatures that have total power 8000 or less.

"I've invested a fun new weight-loss machine! It's guaranteed to make you thinner, or your money back!"
—Rikoho, the Dismantler

6 Armored Transport Galiacruse
ARMORLOID

- Instead of having this creature attack, you may tap it to use its ⊕ ability.
- ⊕ Each of your fire creatures gets "This creature can attack untapped creatures" until the end of the turn.

Luckily, it doesn't rely on the element of surprise.

5000

5 Astronaut Skyterror
ARMORED WYVERN

- While you have no other creatures in the battle zone, this creature has "Power attacker +4000 (While attacking, this creature gets +4000 power)" and "Double breaker (This creature breaks 2 shields)."

"In case of emergency, you're in deep trouble."

4000+

3 Cratersaur
ROCK BEAST

- While you have no shields, this creature can attack untapped creatures and has "Power attacker +3000 (While attacking, this creature gets +3000 power)."

"Uh oh—I'm erupting again."

2000+

3 Energy Charger

- One of your creatures gets +2000 power until the end of the turn.
- Charger (After you cast this spell, put it into your mana zone instead of your graveyard.)

"Prepare the lava injection!" —Sky Crusher, the Agitator

5 Gazarias Dragon
ARMORED DRAGON

- While you have no shields, this creature gets +4000 power and has "Double breaker (This creature breaks 2 shields)."

"My enemies never know what I'll do next. And neither do I!"

4000+

6 Kipo's Contraption
XENOPARTS

- Instead of having this creature attack, you may tap it to use its ⊕ ability.
- ⊕ Destroy one of your opponent's creatures that has power 2000 or less.

"Safety inspector? What's that?" —Engineer Kipo

3000

2 Kooc Pollon
FIRE BIRD

- This creature can't be attacked.

To Fire Birds, a battlefield and a playground are one and the same.

1000

6 Otherworldly Warrior Naghi
ARMORLOID

- This creature can't be attacked.
- Power attacker +3000 (While attacking, this creature gets +3000 power.)
- Double breaker (This creature breaks 2 shields.)

It's a gnabbin', dribin', cleavin', smashin', shootin', stompin' fighter.

4000+

7 Sky Crusher, the Agitator
DRAGONOID

- Instead of having this creature attack, you may tap it to use its ⊕ ability.
- ⊕ Each player puts a card from his mana zone into his graveyard.

Firing goes a lot faster when you don't have that pesky readying and aiming.

4000

6 Valkrowzer, Ultra Rock Beast
ROCK BEAST

- Evolution—Put one of your Rock Beasts.
- Water stealth (This creature can't be blocked while your opponent has no water cards in his mana zone.)
- Double breaker (This creature breaks 2 shields.)

"I liked him better when he was dormant." —Topira

9000

3 Wild Racer Chief Garan
HUNTER

- Power attacker +1000 (While attacking, this creature gets +3000 power.)
- Light stealth (This creature can't be blocked while your opponent has any light cards in his mana zone.)

Burning rubber, burning rage.

2000+

73

4 — Brood Shell
COLONY BEETLE

3000

- Instead of having this creature attack, you may tap it to use its ⊕ ability.
- ⊕ Return a creature from your mana zone to your hand.

Colony Beetles do nothing but lay eggs, ponder the existential questions of truth and beauty, and lay more eggs.

6 — Cryptic Totem
MYSTERY TOTEM

6000

- Double breaker (This creature breaks 2 shields.)
- While this creature is tapped, your opponent can't use the "shield trigger" ability of his shields.

"He speaks in riddles. Or gibberish. I can't tell." —Fighter Dual Fang

3 — Freezing Icehammer
SPELL

- Choose one of your opponent's water or darkness creatures in the battle zone. Your opponent puts that creature into his mana zone.

"Freeze 'em and squeeze 'em!" —Gordoon, the Glider

4 — Fruit of Eternity
SPELL

- Shield trigger (When this spell is put into your hand from your shield zone, you may cast it immediately for no cost.)
- Whenever any of your creatures would be destroyed this turn, put it into your mana zone instead.

9 — Headlong Giant
GIANT

14000

- This creature can't attack if you have no cards in your hand.
- Whenever this creature attacks, discard a card from your hand.
- This creature can't be blocked by any creature that has power 4000 or less.
- Triple breaker (This creature breaks 3 shields.)

3 — Launch Locust
GIANT INSECT

2000+

- While attacking, this creature gets +1000 power for each other creature you have in the battle zone.

It's great for mashing mosquitos, scaring off skyterrors, and putting on totally awesome fireworks displays.

3 — Mulch Charger
SPELL

- Put one of your creatures from the battle zone into your mana zone.
- Charger (After you cast this spell, put it into your mana zone instead of your graveyard.)

Its bark is boing; its sap is blood. Its leaves are real leaves, though.

4 — Popple, Flowerpetal Dancer
SNOW FAERIE

2000

- Instead of having this creature attack, you may tap it to use its ⊕ ability.
- ⊕ Put the top card of your deck into your mana zone.

"I wish every day was the first day of spring. Hold on—I have magical powers! I can just do that!"

5 — Spinning Totem
MYSTERY TOTEM

4000

- Instead of having this creature attack, you may tap it to use its ⊕ ability.
- ⊕ This turn, whenever any of your nature creatures is attacking your opponent and becomes blocked, it breaks one of his shields. (If a creature has "double breaker" or "triple breaker," it still breaks only one shield.)

4 — Stinger Horn, the Delver
HORNED BEAST

3000+

- Power attacker +1000 (While attacking, this creature gets +1000 power.)
- Water stealth (This creature can't be blocked while your opponent has any water cards in his mana zone.)

"See? The swimming lessons worked!" —Fear Fang

4 — Tangle Fist, the Weaver
BEAST FOLK

2000

- Instead of having this creature attack, you may tap it to use its ⊕ ability.
- ⊕ Put up to 3 cards from your hand into your mana zone.

Few shamans study the craft of gaga magic; fewer still become masters.

6 — World Tree, Root of Life
TREE FOLK

7000+

- Evolution—Put on one of your Tree Folk.
- Power attacker +2000 (While attacking, this creature gets +2000 power.)
- Darkness stealth (This creature can't be blocked while your opponent has any darkness cards in his mana zone.)
- Double breaker (This creature breaks 2 shields.)

Dracobarrier

3

(Illus. Junza)

- Shield trigger *(When this spell is put into your hand from one of your shields, you may cast it immediately for no cost.)*
- Choose one of your opponent's creatures in the battle zone and tap it. If it has Dragon in its race, add the top card of your deck to your shields face down.

©2005 Wizards of the Coast
Shogakukan/Mitsui-Kids   6/55

Kuukai, Finder of Karma

5

MECHA THUNDER

(Illus. Yamadora)

EVOLUTION CREATURE

- Blocker *(Whenever an opponent's creature attacks, you may tap this creature to stop the attack. Then the 2 creatures battle.)*
- Evolution—Put on one of your Mecha Thunders.
- Whenever this creature blocks, untap it after it battles.
- This creature can't attack players.

10500

©2005 Wizards of the Coast
Shogakukan/Mitsui-Kids   7/55

Laser Whip

4

(Illus. Takimi Nano)

SPELL

- Choose one of your opponent's creatures in the battle zone and tap it. Then you may choose one of your creatures in the battle zone. If you do, it can't be blocked this turn.

"No, no, no! It's not a laser! It's a high-intensity, focused, optical beam! Of course, it emits a laser to work." —Datti, Vizier of Restoration

©2005 Wizards of the Coast
Shogakukan/Mitsui-Kids   7/55

Lunar Charger

3

(Illus. Akira Harvesta)

SPELL

- Choose up to 2 of your creatures in the battle zone. At the end of the turn, you may untap them.
- Charger *(After you cast this spell, put it into your mana zone instead of your graveyard.)*

Grotha loved bouncing staff off of walls. That night, the walls had their revenge.

©2005 Wizards of the Coast
Shogakukan/Mitsui-Kids   8/55

Migalo, Vizier of Spycraft

2

INITIATE

(Illus. Junza)

CREATURE

- Turbo rush *(If any of your other creatures broke any shields this turn, this creature gets its ⚡ ability until the end of the turn.)*
- ⚡ Whenever this creature attacks, you may look at 2 of your opponent's shields. Then put them back where they were.

1500

©2005 Wizards of the Coast
Shogakukan/Mitsui-Kids   9/55

Misha, Channeler of Suns

5

MECHA DEL SOL

(Illus. Zenn Hatodeli)

CREATURE

- This creature can't be attacked by any creature that has Dragon in its race.

Once the Dragons awoke, so did the Dragon hunters. The Dragon photographers woke up next, followed closely by the Dragon dentists, Dragon insurance agents, and Dragon souvenir-shop owners.

5000

©2005 Wizards of the Coast
Shogakukan/Mitsui-Kids   15/55

Nariel, the Oracle

4

LIGHT BRINGER

(Illus. Atsushi Kawarai)

CREATURE

- Creatures that have power 3000 or more can't attack. *(Creatures that have power less than 3000 and get extra power while attacking can still attack.)*

Just as predicted, the earthquakes created by the waking Dragons reactivated the sentinels. Everything was still under their control.

1000

©2005 Wizards of the Coast
Shogakukan/Mitsui-Kids   13/55

Nastasha, Channeler of Suns

7

MECHA DEL SOL

(Illus. Masaki Hirooka)

CREATURE

- Double breaker *(This creature breaks 2 shields.)*
- When one of your shields would be broken, you may destroy this creature instead.

The universe trembles at its bequest.

8000

©2005 Wizards of the Coast
Shogakukan/Mitsui-Kids   12/55

Sasha, Channeler of Suns

8

MECHA DEL SOL

(Illus. Junza)

CREATURE

- 🔵 Dragon blocker *(Whenever an opponent's creature that has Dragon in its race attacks, you may tap this creature to stop the attack. Then the 2 creatures battle.)*
- While battling a creature that has Dragon in its race, this creature gets +6000 power.
- Double breaker *(This creature breaks 2 shields.)*

9500+

©2005 Wizards of the Coast
Shogakukan/Mitsui-Kids   13/55

Solar Grass

5

STARLIGHT TREE

(Illus. Kudoshiki Kojin)

CREATURE

- Turbo rush *(If any of your other creatures broke any shields this turn, this creature gets its ⚡ ability until the end of the turn.)*
- ⚡ Whenever this creature is attacking your opponent and isn't blocked, untap all your creatures in the battle zone except Solar Grasses.

3000

©2005 Wizards of the Coast
Shogakukan/Mitsui-Kids   14/55

Sol Galla, Halo Guardian

2

GUARDIAN

(Illus. Jinn Pat)

CREATURE

- Blocker *(Whenever an opponent's creature attacks, you may tap this creature to stop the attack. Then the 2 creatures battle.)*
- Whenever a player casts a spell, this creature gets +3000 power until the end of the turn. *(So when the spell says before this creature gets the extra power.)*

1000+

©2005 Wizards of the Coast
Shogakukan/Mitsui-Kids   13/55

Thrumiss, Zephyr Guardian

6

GUARDIAN

(Illus. Hiroaki Morooka)

CREATURE

- Whenever any of your creatures attacks, you may choose one of your opponent's creatures in the battle zone and tap it. *(First choose what your creature is attacking. Then choose a creature to tap.)*

"Catch my drift?"

3000

©2005 Wizards of the Coast
Shogakukan/Mitsui-Kids   15/55

Aqua Grappler
5
LIQUID PEOPLE

CREATURE

- Whenever this creature attacks, you may draw a card for each other tapped creature you have in the battle zone.

"I specialize in locking! And jumping! And sometimes spinning and whirling! I know my team will all that money on grappling lessons, but that's just not what I'm into anymore."

3000

Aqua Ranger
6
LIQUID PEOPLE

CREATURE

- This creature can't be blocked.
- When this creature would be destroyed, put it into your hand instead.

"I'm on a special mission to the surface to bring back secret computer codes, enemy troop movements, and a case of metal polish."

3000

Candy Cluster
3
CYBER CLUSTER

CREATURE

- This creature can't be blocked.

Its crunchy outer shell protects a creamy caramel center.

1000

Emperor Quazla
6
CYBER LORD

EVOLUTION CREATURE

- Blocker (Whenever an opponent's creature attacks, you may tap this creature to stop the attack. Then the 2 creatures battle.)
- Evolution—Put on one of your Cyber Lords.
- Whenever your opponent uses the "shield trigger" ability of one of his shields, draw 2 cards.

5000

Eureka Charger
4
SPELL

- Draw a card.
- Charger (After you cast this spell, put it into your mana zone instead of your graveyard.)

"The expansion is touch for the stars," not "reach for the mysterious bolt of crackling electricity." —Mighty Bandit

Grape Globbo
2
CYBER VIRUS

CREATURE

- When you put this creature into the battle zone, look at your opponent's hand.

"I'm quite fully protected from telepathic spies. Indeed, that's what my saffy hat is for. Who-hoi!!!"
—Quazla Hero Swine Scout

1000

Illusion Fish
4
GEL FISH

CREATURE

- Turbo rush (If any of your other creatures broke any shields this turn, this creature gets its ⬡ ability until the end of the turn.)
  ⬡ This creature can't be blocked.

"Watch closely for the end of history." —Emperor Quazla

3000

Lalicious
6
SEA HACKER

CREATURE

- Whenever this creature attacks, look at your opponent's hand and at the top card of his deck.

Its artificial eye has X-ray vision, Y-ray vision, and Z-ray vision.

4000

Marine Scramble
7
SPELL

- Your creatures in the battle zone can't be blocked this turn.

"Analysis complete. Begin the assault!" —Emperor Quazla

Prowling Elephish
4
GEL FISH

CREATURE

- Blocker (Whenever an opponent's creature attacks, you may tap this creature to stop the attack. Then the 2 creatures battle.)

"I knew the laws of nature could bend. I didn't know they could be twisted into a pretzel." —Mini Titan Setti

2000

Vikorakys
3
SEA HACKER

CREATURE

- Turbo rush (If any of your other creatures broke any shields this turn, this creature gets its ⬡ ability until the end of the turn.)
  ⬡ When this creature attacks, search your deck. You may take a card from your deck and put it into your hand. Then shuffle your deck.

1000

Wave Lance
3
SPELL

- Choose a creature in the battle zone and return it to its owner's hand. If it has Dragon in its race, you may draw a card.

Even the rulers of the skies cannot best the waters.

4 Corpse Charger

SPELL

- Put a creature from your graveyard into your hand.
- Charger (After you cast this spell, put it into your mana zone instead of your graveyard.)

The dead rose from their graves and began their slow march into the swamp. Only Argus wondered who would feed his worms while he was away.

4 Cranium Clamp

SPELL

- Your opponent chooses and discards 2 cards from his hand.

"Hold still! This is the only headache remedy I know. I promise, soon you won't be able to feel your head at all!"

3 Dimension Splitter
BRAIN JACKER

CREATURE

- When you put this creature into the battle zone, you may return all creatures that have Dragon in their race from your graveyard to your hand.

They think life is a joke, death is a joke, and mixing the two up is a really funny joke.

1000

3 Gachack, Mechanical Doll
DEATH PUPPET

CREATURE

- Turbo rush (If any of your other creatures broke any shields this turn, this creature gets its ability until the end of the turn.)
- Whenever this creature is attacking your opponent and isn't blocked, you may destroy a creature.

2000

5 Gigaclaws
CHIMERA

CREATURE

- Turbo rush (If any of your other creatures broke any shields this turn, this creature gets its ability until the end of the turn.)
- Whenever this creature attacks, your opponent discards his hand.

2000

5 Megaria, Empress of Dread
DARK LORD

CREATURE

- Each creature in the battle zone has "slayer." (Whenever a creature that has "slayer" battles, destroy the other creature after the battle.)

Before the early client army, she raised the chalice of souls. "This time," she snarled. "It better be filled with dirt souls."

5000

4 Motorcycle Mutant
HEDRIAN

CREATURE

- Blocker (Whenever an opponent's creature attacks, you may tap this creature to stop the attack. Then the 2 creatures battle.)
- This creature can't attack.
- When you put another creature into the battle zone, destroy this creature.

6000

6 Necrodragon Galbazeek
ZOMBIE DRAGON

CREATURE

- Whenever this creature attacks, choose one of your shields and put it into your graveyard.
- Double breaker (This creature breaks 2 shields.)

Its wingbeats whisper promises of doom.

9000

4 Necrodragon Giland
ZOMBIE DRAGON

CREATURE

- Double breaker (This creature breaks 2 shields.)
- When this creature battles, destroy it after the battle.

The rescue and regrets of thousands upon thousands united into one entity—and the cursed Dragon stirred from its slumber.

6000

6 Scream Slicer, Shadow of Fear
GHOST

CREATURE

- Whenever you put a Dragonoid or a creature that has Dragon in its race into the battle zone, destroy the creature that has the least power in the battle zone. If there's a tie, you choose from among the tied creatures.

Neither flesh nor blood nor souls can ever slake the thirst of the dead.

4000

6 Super Necrodragon Abzo Dolba
ZOMBIE DRAGON

EVOLUTION CREATURE

- Evolution—Put on one of your creatures that has Dragon in its race.
- This creature gets +2000 power for each creature in your graveyard.
- Triple breaker (This creature breaks 3 shields.)

The Dragon rose. Hopes fell.

11000+

1 Tyrant Worm
PARASITE WORM

CREATURE

- When you put another creature into the battle zone, destroy this creature.

It's scared of scared people.

2000

5 Bruiser Dragon
ARMORED DRAGON

- When this creature is destroyed, choose one of your shields and put it into your graveyard.

"It's a Dragon party! Oh yeah! Time to burn this planet to a crisp!"

5000

4 Furious Onslaught

- Until the end of the turn, each of your Dragonoids in the battle zone are an Armored Dragon in addition to its other races, gets +4000 power, and has "Double breaker (This creature breaks 2 shields.)."

"See what happens when you take your vitamins?"
—Pyrofighter Magnus

5 Kyrstron, Lair Delver
DRAGONOID

- When this creature is destroyed, you may put a creature that has Dragon in its race from your hand into the battle zone.

"Sneak in, grab some Dragon eggs, sneak out, and make into enormous omelet. What could be simpler?"

1000

6 Magmadragon Jagalzor
VOLCANO DRAGON

- Double breaker (This creature breaks 2 shields.)
- Turbo rush (If any of your other creatures broke any of this turn, this creature gets its ability until the end of the turn.)
  Each of your creatures in the battle zone has "speed attacker." (A creature that has "speed attacker" doesn't get summoning sickness.)

6000

4 Magmadragon Melgars
VOLCANO DRAGON

Necrodragon slept main under the swamps. Terradragons hibernated at the rim of the great waterfall. Magmadragons slumbered in baths of boiling rock at the volcanoes' cores. One by one, they woke, rose, and continued their reign of destruction as though millions of years had not passed.

4000

3 Missile Soldier Ultimo
DRAGONOID

- Turbo rush (If any of your other creatures broke any shields this turn, this creature gets its ability until the end of the turn.)
  This creature can attack untapped creatures and has "Power attacker +4000 (While attacking, this creature gets +4000 power)."

2000+

4 Rocketdive Skyterror
ARMORED WYVERN

- This creature can't be attacked.
- This creature can't attack players.
- Power attacker +1000 (While attacking, this creature gets +1000 power.)

"And just when we do all the different kinds of Wyverns that have been asleep in the earth for millions of years woke up." Ba-ka"

5000+

4 Slaphappy Soldier Galback
DRAGONOID

- Turbo rush (If any of your other creatures broke any shields this turn, this creature gets its ability until the end of the turn.)
  Whenever this creature attacks, you may destroy one of your opponent's creatures that has power 4000 or less.

3000

5 Torpedo Skyterror
ARMORED WYVERN

- While attacking, this creature gets +2000 power for each other tapped creature you have in the battle zone.

The Wyverns weren't that excited about the rise of their long-lost cousins—until they saw the chaos and confusion the Dragons caused in the wake.

4000+

3 Totto Pipicchi
FLAME BIRD

- Each creature in the battle zone that has Dragon in its race has "speed attacker." (A creature that has "speed attacker" doesn't get summoning sickness.)

The Fire Birds flitted across the sky, their voices raised in joy. The time of awakening had come at last.

1000

7 Überdragon Bajula
ARMORED DRAGON

- Evolution—Put on one of your creatures that has Dragon in its race.
- Whenever this creature attacks, choose up to 2 cards in your opponent's mana zone. Your opponent puts those cards into their graveyard.
- Triple breaker (This creature breaks 3 shields.)

13000

4 Volcano Charger

- Destroy one of your opponent's creatures that has power 2000 or less.
- Charger (After you cast this spell, put it into your mana zone instead of your graveyard.)

Crimson petals scar the earth, sowing the seeds for the next eruption.

EPIC DRAGONS OF HYPERCHAOS (nature)

Bakkra Horn, the Silent — 4
HORNED BEAST

- Whenever you put a Dragonoid or a creature that has Dragon in its race into the battle zone, put the top card of your deck into your mana zone.

Breaking the ancient oath, it led the way to the waterfall where the Terradragons lay dreaming.

2000

Carbonite Scarab — 4
GIANT INSECT

- Turbo rush (If any of your other creatures broke any shields this turn, this creature gets its ability until the end of the turn.)
- Whenever this creature is attacking your opponent and becomes blocked, it breaks one of your opponent's shields.

3000

Coliseum Shell — 4
COLONY BEETLE

- Whenever this creature becomes blocked, you may put the top card of your deck into your mana zone.

"What a terrible, senseless tragedy! My flagshell loss was winning." —Bottom, Master of Death

3000

Dracodance Totem — 2
MYSTERY TOTEM

- When this creature would be destroyed, if you have a creature that has Dragon in its race in your mana zone, put this creature into your mana zone instead of destroying it. Then return a creature that has Dragon in its race from your mana zone to your hand.

1000

Kachua, Keeper of the Icegate — 7
SNOW FAERIE

- Instead of having this creature attack, you may tap it to use its ability.
- Search your deck. You may take a creature that has Dragon in its race from your deck and put it into the battle zone. Then shuffle your deck. That creature has "speed attacker." At the end of the turn, destroy it.

3000

Muscle Charger — 3

- Each of your creatures in the battle zone gets +3000 power until the end of the turn.
- Charges (After you cast this spell, put it into your mana zone instead of your graveyard.)

"Step 1: Prepare for adventures. Who-hoo!!!" —Quixotic Hero Swine Snout

Quixotic Hero Swine Snout — 2
BEAST FOLK

- Whenever another creature is put into the battle zone, this creature gets +3000 power until the end of the turn.

"Note Nattie, my piggy steed. This pesky no-brake steed not delay us from our adventures too with the sidbar. Whee-hoo!!!"

1000+

Root Charger — 3
SPELL

- Whenever any of your creatures would be destroyed this turn, put it into your mana zone instead.
- Charges (After you cast this spell, put it into your mana zone instead of your graveyard.)

Life is the building block of life.

Senia, Orchard Avenger — 4
TREE FOLK

- Turbo rush (If any of your other creatures broke any shields this turn, this creature gets its ability until the end of the turn.)
- This creature gets +5000 power and has "Double breaker (This creature breaks 2 shields)."

Whole armies have been lost on fruit-salad expeditions.

3000+

Super Terradragon Bailas Gale — 5
EARTH DRAGON

- Evolution—Put one of your creatures that has Dragon in its race.
- After you lost a card bearing its "shield trigger" ability, put it into your hand instead if your graveyard.
- Double breaker (This creature breaks 2 shields).

9000

Terradragon Gamiratar — 4
EARTH DRAGON

- When you put this creature into the battle zone, your opponent may choose a creature in his hand and put it into the battle zone.
- Double breaker (This creature breaks 2 shields).

Gamila's doomsday device caused the planet's core to crack. That was the same clock the Dragons had been waiting for.

6000

Terradragon Regarion — 5
EARTH DRAGON

- Power attacker +3000 (While attacking, this creature gets +3000 power.)
- Double breaker (This creature breaks 2 shields.)

Once the Gate of Words was something's destroyed, there was nothing that could hold the Dragons back.

4000+

Create the biggest, baddest, most awesomest DUEL MASTERS creature and it could be featured as an exclusive Duel Masters card.

Unleash Your Inner Creature

To enter visit www.duelmasters.com or call 1-800-324-6496 for more information.

DUEL MASTERS
Unleash your inner creature tod